A MOUTH FULL OF SALT

Reem Gaafar

A Mouth
Full of Salt

SAQI

SAQI BOOKS
Gable House, 18–24 Turnham Green Terrace
London W4 1QP
www.saqibooks.com

Published in Great Britain by Saqi Books in 2024

ISBN 978 0 86356 772 8
eISBN 978 0 86356 748 3

Printed and bound by Clays Ltd, Elcograf S.p.A

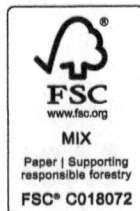

FSC
www.fsc.org
MIX
Paper | Supporting
responsible forestry
FSC® C018072

For my family, and for Abdelrahman

Part I

One

Until a body was actually found, they referred to him as 'missing'. But they went about their business of looking for someone who was dead, not alive. They weren't looking for a boy, they were looking for a body. It was the same with everyone: they were someone, with a name, until they died or were presumed dead. Then they were immediately referred to as 'The Body'.

First, they brought in skilled swimmers who combed the river from bank to bank, swimming with the current for several metres and then turning against it back to where the person was last seen. Diving deep below the surface, where the sunlight of the living world stopped short a few feet in and gave way to murky, morbid darkness, they fanned blindly around with their eyes wide open, their experienced fingers discerning root and fish from human limb or clothing. Experience taught them that bodies almost always stayed in the area where they drowned, often held down by tree roots and thick rushes like ropes, and would be found within a four or five-metre radius of where the person had fallen in.

Then, if still no body materialised, they would call for a pusher-tug boat from the River Transport Corporation headquarters upstream in the town of Karima. These little vessels, which were used to tow the bigger barges into port when they were brought in for maintenance, had powerful engines and greatly elevated the search efforts. It usually took some personal connections to secure a tug and its driver for a few hours, for their village was small and far away and the Corporation was a busy place. However at this time of year, during the low-water period between February and March, the tugboat's services could be acquired with little effort, as traffic was slow in the Dongola Reach between Karima and Dongola. Also, the war waged on in the South, all but shutting down the Southern Reach between Kosti and Juba where the South Sudanese rebels kept sinking the passing steamers. The tugboat would chug around the perimeter of the area where the body was last seen, its powerful engine churning the water and agitating the river floor. Up would come the mud, the weeds, the fish, and – if they were lucky – the body. Back and forth the noisy tugboat would go, pulling up behind it all that slept at the bottom of the river.

Calls were made to villages downstream, alerting the neighbours to look out for a boy/girl/man/woman of so-and-so physical description, the son/daughter of so-and-so family. If the missing person wasn't found on the first day, people would take turns to camp around the area and wait for the body to float. The putrefaction process usually took around 48 hours, during which time the intestines filled with gas, strong enough to release the person from whatever was holding them down and allow them to drift up to the surface. Then, wherever they were found, they would be buried, because – as everyone knows – drowned bodies cannot be handled after spending long periods of time in water: the skin becomes friable and rips easily. The bodies are pulled carefully from the water and placed straight into waiting graves that would be dug a short distance away, and prayed over without washing or shrouding. There are several graveyards along the sides of the river coinciding with the shallowest and most turbulent parts of the Nile, where bodies carried downstream are pushed to the surface and caught in place by protruding tree roots and rocks. For as long as people can remember, families from the villages along the Nile travel long distances to pray over their loved ones' graves, miles away from where they should have been buried, had they died a natural death. It is a tradition as old as the Nile itself, and a fate that is intertwined with the fabric of those living alongside the great river.

The villagers had been diving and swimming since the early morning and the villages downstream had already been alerted to look out for the boy who had gone missing. Men lined the banks of the Nile on both sides, watching the swimmers dipping in and out of the water. The burning sun was moving toward the middle of the sky and the men's shadows shortened to meet their feet as if they were trying to hide from the heat underneath their jallabiyas. Several young men were stripped down to their waists. They stood over the banks, flexing and waiting for their turn in the water, or lay on their backs, stretching their aching limbs after their swimming shift. The search had begun several long hours ago and discussions were already underway about who would take the first shift camping on the bank that evening, and who would take over tomorrow. The men knew – from long, painful experience – that if a boy this small had not been found at this point then he would most likely be stuck inside a sinkhole deep in the river bed. They compared this drowning to others, counting the hours or days it had taken for each past body to be found.

'My brother only floated on the fourth day. We thought he had been eaten by crocodiles.'

'Not unheard of – though thankfully crocodiles have more or less disappeared from these waters now.'

'–Four whole days until we had a body to bury! My poor mother was never the same again, may Allah have mercy on her soul. I remember it like it was yesterday.'

'We'll keep looking until the sun sets but we can't keep the tugboat for more than another hour.'

Opinions appeared to rank in importance and authority according to the size and height of the speaker's turban. The last words were spoken by the man with the largest turban and drew murmurs of assent from the crowd, with one or two men repeating that the tug could not be kept for too long. The man drew even more importance from the fact that it was he who had secured the boat's services – free, of course, as no one would accept payment for such a sad service.

The missing boy's father stood silently a short distance away from the group of men and boys, his hands clasped behind his back, staring into the water from under thick, black eyebrows. He wore only a cap on his head – no turban – and did not join in the discussion. Between the cap and the left eyebrow, a jagged scar climbed across his temple and parted the hair on the side of his head. The villagers did not invite him to join them nor asked his opinion, only glanced in his direction occasionally, raising their voices so that their discussion was heard, pausing briefly after each suggestion was put forth, awaiting approval or refusal. Neither was offered and so they went on with their business. On the ground between the men and the father were the missing boy's abandoned sandals and his crumpled clothes. One sandal lay on its side, betraying its owner's haste to jump into the water that morning.

❧

Fatima leaned against the abandoned pigeon house that stood on the hill at the highest point of the village. It gave the clearest view of the terrain below; the line where the houses stopped and date tree gardens began, and where the gardens gave way to the river. She strained her neck to try and catch a glimpse of the men in the water, but the tree line obscured her view. She had been standing there for almost half an hour, picking up the snippets of conversation carried by the breeze from the riverside that gave her some idea of the progress – or lack thereof – of the search. She heard the diesel-fuelled chugging of the tugboat in wafts and waves, and how the engine churned every time the driver revved it. She hated that sound: it reminded her of past nauseating trips across the river on the ferry where she had stood at the end of the flat bed with the other women, while the ferry dipped deep into the water whenever a large truck backed onto it, threatening to tip over. Judging by the muted tone and continuous splashing, there was nothing new in the search for the missing boy.

Fatima was bored and tired, and the heat was becoming unbearable. The fractured shade of the pigeon house provided little protection from the sun, and the small building was surrounded by rocks and fallen walls which housed all sorts of pests, including scorpions. They were all hiding in their holes from the heat at the moment, but

Fatima knew that the promise of fresh blood offered by her exposed toes might easily lure them out.

From her vantage point, Fatima could see clearly into the front and back yards of the houses below her. Even though she knew it was rude and she should avert her gaze, she followed some of the occupants with guilty interest. There was old Haj Yousif, hobbling wearily on his crooked legs across the front yard towards the outhouse. She watched him support himself against the wall as he paced forward, then abandoned his mission and turned instead towards his daughter's henna bushes to empty his bladder. Fatima giggled and looked away in embarrassment, wondering if the women who bought the dried and powdered henna from Hasina knew that the plant was watered with the old man's urine. A few houses down she could see Fathiya bit Zainab, hanging up clothes to dry. Her fat arms wobbled visibly even from that distance. Fathiya was married to one of Fatima's many uncles and she had no children of her own – at least not anymore. She was always complaining about what a nuisance Haj Adam was becoming now that he was hard of hearing, getting more stubborn by the year, and how her family had married her off to someone twice her age. Then she would hurry home to get his lunch ready and put the hot coals in the incense burner, so that when he came home the house smelled nice and his food was hot, because 'he won't eat anything that isn't cooked by me,' she would say happily.

Fatima's house was adjacent to Fathiya's, separated by a narrow alley. Even though only the roof was visible from where she stood, Fatima knew that there wouldn't be anyone in the yard to see. Her father had rushed out of the house early that morning as soon as he had heard the news and hadn't returned for either breakfast or lunch, and her mother would be in the kitchen preparing the lunch trays that would be taken down to the men by the river. Fatima had helped her cook the lamb stew and gurasa and had arranged the dishes on the trays before her mother had sent her off to see if Sulafa had arrived – an errand she had accepted with both relief and irritation. She was happy to be released from the hot kitchen and endless housework, but was not looking forward to meeting the missing boy's mother.

Fatima's house, like all the houses on the row, was only half of what it had been before. The eastern wall and the old men's quarters had collapsed in the floods of 1988, less than a year before. There had been another row of houses between Fatima's house and the gardens but those had disappeared completely. The mud walls from which their homes were built kept them cool throughout the hot, dry weather that lasted most of the year but were no match for the flood water that had seeped through the date gardens and stagnated at their foundations, melting the mud bricks until whole buildings collapsed.

Almost a year later, the former occupants of these homes were still displaced on higher ground, staying with relatives as they attempted to piece their homes back together. Some of them had decided to abandon the ruins altogether and relocate. From her vantage point Fatima looked down on a village that was an incomplete copy of the village she had known her whole life, with large chunks of it missing here and there, like a messily amputated limb.

Fatima knew who the missing boy was – everyone did. He was the only son of Sulafa and Hamid Kheir Alseed;

a short, friendly eight-year-old boy with a chipped tooth. His name was Mohamed, and his cousin and two friends were the ones who had reported him missing. They had all been swimming in a shallow area of the river when a sudden current had come from nowhere and swept the boy off. At least, that was the story that the friends and cousin had told, but Fatima knew it was unlikely to be the whole truth, and she was sure everyone else knew so too. The village boys played all sorts of stupid and dangerous games in the Nile. And they played in all sorts of places which they were not supposed to; areas where mini whirlpools regularly materialised, sucking even the most experienced swimmers deep down into the water and keeping them there. Electric eels appeared at certain times of the year in some parts of the river. Even if one was only standing knee deep in the water, a single shock from an eel would drop the victim in, paralysed. The danger was highest during the flood season when the water was high, turbulent and vicious. But even during the dry season – like now – when the level was low and the current sluggish, the murky waters of the Nile hid all sorts of unpleasant surprises in its depths.

But the boys were sticking to their story, and Fatima knew they would be following the search fearfully from behind the trees.

The villagers were no strangers to drowning. None of those who lived in the villages on the banks of the Nile from the far South to the far North were. People of all ages drowned for any number of reasons: a swimming accident, standing on a weak part of the bank that collapsed, suicide, murder, an unpleasant surprise from the depths that dragged someone under. Sometimes senile men and women strayed from their homes at night and fell in. The same river that watered their vegetables and animals, generated their electricity, kept them cool in the hot summer months and transported them wherever they wished to go; that same river swallowed their children and livestock whole whenever one was foolish enough to get too close or become too comfortable with it. The Nile was a trap that attracted, ensnared and buried all at once. It took as much as it gave them and more.

The river brought them life. But the river was not their friend.

Fatima climbed down from the small hill, giving up her watch. Her head was pounding from the heat. She stepped onto the narrow dirt street which wound around the village between the houses and turned north towards Sulafa's in-laws' house, where the missing boy and his parents lived. The sun beat down on her mercilessly from a cloudless sky and she walked close to the walls to catch whatever shade was thrown by the sparse trees behind them.

The sound of the afternoon news bulletin crackled faintly in the air from a radio in one of the houses she passed and the disembodied voice of the Prime Minister floated over the wall and onto the street. As usual, he was calling on his fellow Sudanese brothers and sisters to stay strong and support each other through the difficult times the country was going through. There were fuel shortages, bread shortages, sugar shortages and no cash. The political parties were bickering like children and throwing the blame around, and the newspapers – which Fatima read after her father was done with them and before using them to line the drawers and soak up the frying oil – published long, elaborate opinion pieces by deep thinkers from the Left and Right sharing infinite wisdom about what should be done and by whom. In their remote village, news from the capital usually garnered little interest except when it concerned gasoline availability and prices. But with the worsening economic conditions and spreading poverty, the villagers followed the news closely, hoping to hear that things were changing.

Women and girls trailed down the street to join the rest of the village's women, who were waiting for the boy's mother to return. A few of them were carrying covered trays of food that would be sent down to the river or to feed the guests waiting at the house. Sulafa had been away visiting relatives for the past two days. She had headed home that morning as soon as the news of her missing son had been dispatched. She was expected to arrive in the next hour.

Fatima was dragging her feet. She hated houses of mourning. And the only thing worse than a house of mourning was a house that was waiting for a body to appear because without a body, the actual mourning could not begin or end. The wait for news was far worse than mourning someone who was buried safe and sound in the ground. She walked slowly down the small street and came across Wad Alsafi's two daughters, who emerged from an adjoining alley. They were balancing a large tray between them with a colourful woven cover, the younger one trying to keep her tob from slipping off her shoulder and tripping her up. The tob was her mother's. She was only nine and was too young to own any tobs of her own, but too old to walk around in public without one. Instinctively, Fatima adjusted her own tob – also her mother's – which she was already wearing expertly and which gave her no trouble. It was quite a feat, wearing four and a half metres of cloth around the waist and over the head, wrapped in such a way that it covered the whole body without limiting movement, and Fatima was proud of her expertise.

Coming towards them from the opposite direction was Sit Amna, the butcher's wife and Fatima's school teacher. She was carrying her empty tray home, keen to get it back safely even though her name was written on the underside in bright red nail polish. Almost everyone in the village owned a similar tray, and it might get sent down to the men by the river where it would almost certainly be displaced. As they neared her, the girls called out to Sit Amna in greeting and asked her the same question they'd all been asking one another since news of the missing boy had surfaced, and would continue to ask until he was found.

'Anything new?'

'Nothing yet,' Amna replied, lifting Wad Alsafi's daughter's tob and securing it around the young girl's waist to keep it from slipping. 'Mustafa Wad Homri called and said Sulafa's bus had left Tangasi and will arrive here in about an hour. Enough time for me to get this tray home and get back.'

Spurred on by this news and by the freedom to move faster without the fear of tripping up, the girls picked up their pace to reach the house and find a safe place for their tray before Mohamed's mother arrived and chaos erupted. The mother that would now be referred to as 'mother of None'. Fatima greeted Sit Amna and the latter squeezed her shoulder briefly before hurrying on. Fatima wanted to ask her teacher the same question the girls had asked, but the news she was waiting for was nothing to do with the search and Fatima thought it would be insensitive to talk of it at such a time, so she hurried on. Fatima wanted to have her face seen at the Kheir Alseed household before returning home and letting her mother know that Sulafa had arrived. The family would be distraught by the news of their missing son, but she knew they would still be keeping a sharp eye out for who had come and who hadn't.

As Fatima walked, she listened to the sisters argue about the chores that were waiting for them at home and whose turn it was to do what.

'It's my turn to hang the washing.'

'No, it's not! You hung the washing last time. It's *my* turn to do that and your turn to clean the outhouse.'

Understandably, neither wanted to clean the outhouse.

'I wonder if the school results have arrived. If Sit Amna isn't there who will pick up the phone when they call?'

'Don't be silly, they don't deliver school results over the phone. They send them by telegram.'

'How do you know that?'

'I just know.'

Fatima was wondering and worrying about the end of year school results too. She had sat her final year exams earlier in the Spring and couldn't wait to see how she had done. She knew that the results were delivered by mail – not over the phone or by telegram, of course.

She wondered if the drowned boy and his mother, Sulafa, had been waiting eagerly for the exam results as well.

Two

Sulafa stepped – or rather, collapsed – through the large open gates and was immediately engulfed by the mass of weeping women awaiting her arrival. The house was packed; the younger women filling the front yard and the older women in the shaded veranda where Sulafa's mother-in-law sat. Everyone was there, like at a wedding or a naming celebration, except everyone was crying, or at least pretending to cry. Fatima stood near one of the thick pillars that held up the roof over the veranda, watching Sulafa slowly approach the house, propelled forward from embrace to embrace. Unlike many of the houses in the village where the roofs were plain dried date fronds, the roof in this house was white American zinc supported by thick tree trunks. No water leaked through when it rained – which it rarely did, anyway. The veranda wrapped the whole way around the house and was wide, with a hard stone surface, and the kitchens behind it were as big as Fatima's entire house. The house walls were built of red brick, covered with cement and whitewashed regularly, with and without occasion. They contrasted sharply with the mud walls that held up the houses on either side, which the villagers continuously coated with mud and animal excrement to fill in the cracks.

Fatima glanced at Sulafa's mother-in-law, Hajja Allagiya, who was seated in the middle of the veranda against the wall. She was dressed in full attire complete with jewellery and leather sandals, as if the news of her missing grandson was neither new nor calamitous. Her face was round and shiny with traditional tribal shulookh scars running down her cheeks in three longitudinal lines. Her well-kept hair was a deep orange at the roots, dark black where the plaits twisted around her ears. Despite having been widowed for many years, her hands and feet were adorned with shiny black henna, framed with straight, clean lines. She wore two thick gold bracelets on each wrist, and several rings. She had made no move to meet her daughter-in-law, and neither had any of her daughters who were standing near her. Sulafa, weeping and dragging her tob behind her, limped into the shade of the veranda where she crumpled down into a chair. Her hair stuck to her wet face in clumps. She was missing an earring. She did not look to her in-laws for condolence or support. Her miserable grief contrasted sharply with the celebratory floral henna drawings on her hand and feet, a souvenir of the wedding she had just arrived from. Even over the noise, Fatima heard some girls behind her whispering.

'Look at her.'

She couldn't tell which 'her' they meant, because there were several. Sulafa and Hajja Allagiya, of course. But also, on the far end of the veranda, the only young woman other than Sulafa who was sitting in the shade was Hamid Kheir Alseed's second wife, Sara.

'She isn't even pretending to cry,' the girls hissed.

'She might as well be laughing.'

'She wouldn't dare laugh now, at least not in front of everyone. But she could at least pretend to be sad.'

'Poor Sulafa!'

Indeed, Sara's puffy face was impassive as she looked at Sulafa. Fatima watched her closely, curiously, trying to read the look on the young wife's face. She was one year younger than Fatima but already had two daughters and was now heavily pregnant with twins. That was young even for the village, where girls were sometimes married off before their first blood. It was common for a man to take more than one wife here, but this rarely occurred without the knowledge of the first one and sometimes with her full consent, since the second wife would almost always be from the same village or a neighbouring one. Usually, the first wife outranked the junior one and was given a level of respect from the family and the husband. She would be presented with a new gold set and would keep her original rooms. But in Sulafa's case, the new wife clearly outranked the old, and her in-laws made no secret of their contempt for Sulafa, who had not produced another child for them.

Fatima felt a tap on her shoulder and turned to see her cousin, Sawsan. Her tob was jumbled up from being squashed by the crowd of women as she made her way over to Fatima. Sawsan looked at the two girls whispering behind them with disdain and turned back to Fatima.

'Did you manage to see anything?'

She knew that Fatima would have been up near the pigeon house.

'Nothing,' Fatima replied. 'At least, nothing about Sulafa's son.'

She whispered into Sawsan's ear about Haj Yousif's outhouse misadventure and they stifled their giggles with their clothes, but drew a sharp 'tsk!' from a couple of women next to them anyway. Sawsan adjusted her tob, bringing it up to cover her face so that only her eyes were showing. Every movement she made dispatched a heavy, smoky perfume. Sawsan was soon to be wed. In her pre-wedding confinement, she took twice daily dukhan sessions, smoking her body with scented wood that turned it a dark shade of orange. The strong musk of the wood lingered in the air long after the bride-to-be had passed by. Fatima found the smell nauseating but kept that to herself, enduring the smell whenever they spent time together, which was almost daily. Sawsan hadn't left the house at all during her two months of confinement, but Mohamed's disappearance was considered a special occasion of sorts.

The yard was emptying fast now that Sulafa had arrived. Women and girls embraced her and greeted Hajja Allagiya and the daughters, echoing their wishes for the speedy and safe return of their missing son, then left in singles and groups to hurry home and get lunch ready for their returning husbands and sons. As they got in line to greet Sulafa, Fatima watched the other family members carefully. Next to Hajja Allagiya stood Hayat, her oldest daughter, and on her other side stood Hafsa and Om Salama. Like their mother, the daughters were well-dressed and fully adorned with fat gold ornaments. They always looked like that. Sometimes Fatima wondered if they slept that way, too.

'May Allah return him in full health ya Sulafa.'

Fatima's words landed somewhere over Sulafa's head as she held her limp hand in her own. Sulafa took no notice of her surroundings or of who was talking to her, but behind her the Kheir Alseed women watched every move like a group of hawks. Fatima looked up at them and caught Sara's eye. The latter looked back at her unfalteringly, almost daringly, her face blank. Fatima moved on to greet Hajja Allagiya.

'May Allah return Mohamed in full health.'

'Where's your mother? I don't see her.'

Of course, Fatima thought.

'She's waiting for me to return and she'll be on her way.'

Hajja Allagiya had already turned her attention to the woman behind Fatima, dismissing both her and her absent mother with disinterest. Fatima turned away and headed towards the door where she stood to wait for Sawsan who was once again trapped and wriggling to break free. She saw Hajja Allagiya's approving smile as she took Sawsan's hand in her own. Not only had Sawsan come out of her confinement to pay her respects, but she was soon to join the ranks of the married women: something which raised her above the single girls. Fatima tried and failed to stifle her irritation. Her mother would come later, but she had already been placed on Hajja Allagiya's blacklist.

❧

The sun was setting as Fatima and Sawsan made their way home. Around them, women stepped into houses and disappeared into alleyways, clearing the dusty street. They walked slowly even though they knew they should be hurrying home before the sun set. It was frowned upon for women to roam the streets after dark, and once the air had cooled, scorpions would come out of their hiding places, clicking their poisonous tails and ready for action. Sawsan had missed Sulafa's arrival and wanted to know all the details.

'They didn't even greet her? Not one of them?'

'Not one.'

'Not even Om Salama? She seems to be the nicest one. I've seen her talk to Sulafa a few times in public and she seems, well, normal.'

'Not even Om Salama. She didn't move from her mother's side. What is it with all that gold they insist on wearing?'

Sawsan snorted.

'You know what they're like. Even my mother wears her gold everywhere she goes.'

'Your mother doesn't wear three kilograms of gold in the middle of the afternoon. She doesn't even own half that much.'

'If I owned three kilograms of gold, I would wear it in the middle of the afternoon.'

They laughed, leaning on each other.

'Well then, Omar should get ready. Does he know what high expectations you have?'

'Oh please,' Sawsan rolled her eyes. 'Omar wouldn't be able to pick me out of a crowd if you asked him to, let alone know my likes and dislikes.'

'He doesn't need to; he has his mother and all those sisters to do that for him. It's a good thing they love gold as much as you do.'

Fatima laughed again, but Sawsan did not respond. Fatima glanced at her, wondering if her jokes were not being received well. Fatima knew she sometimes went overboard and not everyone appreciated her sense of humour. But Sawsan rarely took offence, and if Fatima had gone too far, she would usually tell her. Their mothers were sisters and the girls had grown up together, so there was little formality between them.

'Isn't it strange? This whole drowning business today,' Sawsan said in a thoughtful voice.

'What's strange about it? People drown all the time.'

Sawsan had lost more than one cousin to the river, all of whom had known how to swim.

'Yes, I know. I just wonder.'

Fatima did not reply. She had an idea what was on Sawsan's mind but didn't want to draw it out because it irritated her, made her uncomfortable. But she didn't have to say anything because Sawsan spoke her mind anyway.

'Do you think he saw her?'

Fatima didn't answer immediately, but stared at the orange shards advancing across the sky. The pale, cloudless blue that had dominated them all day was being chased behind the mountains and soon all trace of it would be gone; as if it had never been there at all. The reds and pinks and purples would finish their daily display soon, and disappear too. That was what it was always like, ascent and dominance, followed by decline, irrelevance and non-existence.

'That whole thing is nothing more than a fairy tale. Don't think about it.'

'Everyone talks about it.'

'Who's "everyone"? You mean old women who have nothing better to do with their time than gossip and conspire? We live right next to a river which has been swallowing people up since the beginning of existence.'

'But what if it's true?'

'It's not!' Fatima turned towards Sawsan, stopping in her

tracks. 'There is no such thing as prophecies about drowning that come true! So stop thinking about it!'

They glared at each other for several seconds then moved on, walking faster down the street that was now empty. They reached Sawsan's house first. She pushed the small door open and stepped inside, pausing on the threshold to look back at Fatima.

'Don't forget about tomorrow, we're going to—'

'Perfume the clothes with bukhoor, I know I know.'

'The other Fatima and her sisters will be here at eleven. Can you try and come before them so that we can hide the fancy stuff? I don't want them ruining anything.'

'I'll be here by ten.'

Sawsan turned back and stepped inside.

'Sawsan,' Fatima called after a second's hesitation. She looked back at her. 'Don't think about it. Everything will be fine.'

Sawsan looked at her and did not reply.

Three

Fatima walked briskly down the street towards her house a few blocks away, hurrying under a flock of birds in flight. Several thoughts were rambling around in her head: the news of Mohamed going missing early in the morning and the humiliating way Sulafa was welcomed in her own home by her in-laws. Sawsan's stupid fears and superstitions about drowning. The thought that always came to her mind whenever a drowning occurred in their village: what had been going on in the boy's head as he thrashed around fighting for air? What was he thinking about as he went under the water?

She didn't know why this question bothered her so much. Knowing the answer would probably achieve nothing at all. But it kept coming, and whenever it came, it was not the person who had just drowned she was seeing. It was her brother, Khalid, battling the treacherous waters of Old Dongola, losing the fight and sinking down into the darkness. Khalid, who had been one of the best swimmers in the region and who – if he had still been alive – would have been the first person to be called down to the river to search for Sulafa's son.

Fatima turned a corner and walked down the road leading to her house, cracked mud walls on her left and a line of dense date tree forest on her right. Her mother hadn't appeared at Sulafa's house at all which was strange; but not too strange. Habiba battled her own demons when news of a drowning occurred, and often when it did not. Fatima remembered how worried she had been about Khalid going on that archaeology expedition, even though it was not the first time he had gone on one and not the first time he had been to Old Dongola. The area was known to be safe with relatively calm waters and uneventful river crossings. Habiba had fretted and worried the day before and the whole day after Khalid had left. When the news of his death reached them three days later, she did not greet it with the muted shock she usually expressed on such occasions, but dropped the bucket of water she had been carrying and fell to the ground with her head in her hands screaming, for what she had been worrying about had come true.

A few feet away from the back door of their house, Fatima became aware that someone was walking beside her in the gloom, behind the line of tree trunks to her right. He had been shadowing her for a while, and she stopped and turned around, knowing who it would be. Sadig, her cousin and – according to local tradition – her future husband. He stepped out from behind the trees into the setting sunshine, smiling jauntily. His clothes were brown and crumpled from lying on the ground on all day while Sadig joined the search for the missing boy. Being one of the best local swimmers, he had swum all the way down to the next village and back four times, he told Fatima.

'And did you find him?' Fatima asked, unimpressed.

Sadig's confident smile faltered and he shifted his weight on his feet uncomfortably.

'No,' he mumbled, avoiding her gaze.

Fatima looked at him with annoyance. Her cousin was almost twenty years old, had never completed his education and now worked with his cousin in the camel trade. He was good at his job and good at swimming, but in her opinion, he was otherwise a total idiot. Harmless and relatively benign, Fatima conceded, but an idiot nonetheless. Of course, she had never had an actual discussion with him before.

'So, what are you so happy about then? What is there to brag about?' she snapped, surprising even herself with the harshness of her tone.

He looked up at her in dismay.

'I'm not bragging, I'm just saying … I swam all the way …' He faltered as his thought process disintegrated in the face of Fatima's wrath.

'So what? What good did that do if you didn't find anything? You should be … you should be ashamed of yourself!'

And with that she turned away, hurried down the remaining path to her house, pushed the door open and stepped inside. Sadig stared after his cousin and flinched as she slammed the door shut. He scratched his head nervously, looked around fearing someone had witnessed the encounter, then slinked back into the trees.

Fatima stood in the front yard with her back against the door, breathing heavily. She was surprised by her behaviour. She had never spoken that way with her cousin before, or with any other male member of her family or community. This wasn't the kind of village where girls spoke freely in the presence of men. It wasn't even the kind of village where girls and women walked in public with men; the small back alleys and streets that lined the houses were how they got about, staying out of the men's way as much as possible. She stood in place for a few minutes wondering if Sadig would come crashing through the door to teach her a lesson, but he didn't, of course. She pushed away and walked across the yard towards the water stand where the water pots stood in the small, elongated cement hut, shaded by a large lemon tree with branches hanging over the sides, scratching anyone who stepped through the narrow entryway. Someone should trim those branches before they poked an eye out, her father often said, but made no move to do it himself. Fatima picked up the steel cup from the bench, reached high over the rim of the clay pot and dipped it into the opening, scooping out some cool water. As she drank, she curled her nose at the flavour of the water. It was subtle, not so unpleasant as to make it undrinkable, but sour enough to remind anyone how bad the water quality was. It hadn't always been this way; it seemed to have changed after the floods.

Fatima found her mother in the kitchen, sitting on the low rope bed where the trays of sliced onions and okra were usually put to dry. Habiba was sitting bent over, with her head low and her back to the main door, facing the small opening leading to the backyard where the wire clotheslines danced loosely in the evening breeze. There were two round food trays on the low stools in front of her, both covered, which Fatima knew were supposed to have been sent down to the river for the men's lunch that afternoon but which obviously had not. The kitchen was tidy and all the pots and pans had been washed and dried, the small cement counter wiped clean and the air was cool; the fires had been put out a while ago. The clotheslines in the alley were empty; all the clothes had been taken down, folded and put away for ironing. Habiba had apparently finished every chore in the house – even Fatima's.

The sudden sound of the call to prayer coming from the small mosque down the road made them both start. The muezzin usually cleared his throat and tapped the microphone before he started, but today he began immediately. His voice was soon joined by other voices from farther away, along with the sound of metal doors opening and closing and footsteps as the men and boys headed down the path alongside the short walls towards the mosque for evening group prayer. The sound from the mosque closest to them died down, echoing slightly against the walls of the neighbourhood. The prayers began and continued for a few more minutes; the imam of their mosque was getting old and had a bad back, so he prayed with very short verses and shot through the kneeling movements as fast as he could.

Sure enough, soon the sound of footsteps and men's voices returned, louder than before as they left the mosque and headed in their respective directions. Some of them loitered around, and the same question was asked in different ways. Any news?

Habiba seemed to come to life and lifted her head, listening for the answer.

No news. The search had been stopped for the day. The first shift out looking – not for a survivor, but for a floating body – had begun. At daybreak the swimmers would begin again, and three more from villages downstream would join them.

'It might be a good idea to bring the tug in again for

an hour or two,' they heard Mustafa, the butcher and Sit Amna's husband, say.

'Aye, maybe we should do that. Hassan is a good chap and always keen to help. But we should be paying him for his time and for the gasoline.'

'That's the least we could do. I told them to pay him today but he refused.'

'And who exactly will be paying? Will the money come out of the cooperative fund? Or from somewhere or someone else?'

The discussion stopped abruptly, as if interrupted. Then:

'Hamid, I didn't see you there. How are you?'

This greeting was met with silence. A couple of other men picked up awkwardly:

'It's a difficult time but God willing we will find him soon,' and, 'Keep reading Yaseen, Allah will light our vision soon.'

A low reply was heard, followed by more awkward silence and then the sound of footsteps as the men quickly dispersed. Fatima was not surprised at this one-sided dialogue and the less-than-friendly reply; Hamid Hassan Kheir Alseed – the missing boy's father and Sulafa's husband – was one of the least popular men in the village. He was arrogant, foul-mouthed and shared his mother's disdain for everyone and everything. His father and uncles had also been despised in their lifetimes and were even rumoured to have killed someone. It was awkward for the village members to help Hamid search for his son with the open animosity between them, but in such matters, it didn't matter whose son it was who was missing – even if it was the village arsehole.

Fatima wondered – not for the first time – what kind of life Sulafa had, with this man for a husband, and his family for in-laws. Hajja Allagiya was known to openly berate Sulafa in front of people for the smallest mistakes as if she was a child. She complained loudly about her daughter-in-law's inability to produce another child; it had been eight years since her son had been born – the son that was now at the bottom of the river. It had grown worse when Sara joined the household and immediately produced two daughters, then soon after became pregnant with twins.

Gloom collected around mother and daughter, each lost in her thoughts, until the sound of the front door opening and slamming shut brought them back to reality. Habiba stood up and turned around to face the door.

'Fatima?' She said in surprise. She hadn't noticed her daughter standing there at all.

Fatima's father stood in the kitchen doorway, peering at his daughter and wife in the low light. They had forgotten to light the kerosene lamps in the kitchen. Mohamed Altahir looked silently down at the covered trays, then up at his wife, a question on his face. Habiba looked down at her hands.

'I sent Abdallah up here five hours ago about these lunch trays,' he said. Fatima pressed her back against the kitchen wall, trying to disappear. She looked at the gap between her father and the door. Too small to slip out of, and her mother was blocking the other exit out into the alleyway.

'The trays weren't ready when he came and I couldn't find anyone to send to the bakery,' Habiba said, still avoiding his eyes. 'I told him to get the bread and come back for the trays but he never did.'

She could have found someone else to take the trays other than Sadig's little brother, Fatima knew. She was sure her father knew this as well.

Mohamed Altahir looked at his wife in silence and after a while she looked up from her hands and held his gaze. This time Fatima contemplated escape out of embarrassment at being caught in the intimacy of their wordless conversation. Though neither parent had opened their mouth, they were talking about Khalid. She had always felt excluded from the collective feeling of loss her brother had left behind. She was told more than once that the loss of a child, being left behind by the person who was supposed to support you in your old age and bury you when you were dead, was nothing like the loss of a sibling, or parent. That feeling was compounded by the lack of a grave to cry at, to visit on Fridays and Eid mornings, to pray over and spray with cool water and arrange green date fronds on. Like all drowned bodies, her brother had been buried by the river far away, next to where he had drowned and where his body had surfaced. They had only visited the site three times in those years since his passing.

Mohamed Altahir opened his mouth to say something, then closed it again. He tapped his fingers against his hand behind his back, looking at the wall over Habiba's head. Then he turned on his heel abruptly and left the kitchen. He stopped a few steps beyond the threshold and turned to look back at them both through the doorway.

'We'll find him soon enough.'

And he turned back around and walked away.

Fatima let out the breath she had been holding, looking at the white apparition of her father dissolving into the dark yard. She cautiously glanced at her mother, saw the blank grief in her face, and felt her soul shrivel up. Habiba stood still, staring into nothing. Her eyes glistened as tears spilled down her thin face. There was only space for one drowned boy in her mother's mind. And it wasn't Sulafa's son.

Four

It was true, Sadig thought to himself wretchedly as he lay on his back under the evening sky. He had nothing to be happy about. He hadn't found the boy. In fact, he had never found any of the drowned people he had been called to search for before. It was always someone else swimming near him who would find the body, and he would rise to the surface alongside them, calling out to those waiting on the riverside and sharing or taking credit that was not his. Because unlike the others, Sadig swam underwater with his eyes tightly shut. Unlike the others, Sadig was terrified of what he would find at the bottom of the river. The thought of touching that clammy skin or looking into a pair of unseeing eyes staring at him through the gloom petrified him. But in the chaos of finding a body people rarely took notice of who was actually holding it. Swimming alongside while calling out loudly was enough to hide the truth: Sadig was a fraud.

As he listened to the boys behind him joking about something or another, his thoughts shifted to his betrothed cousin. Fatima made him uncomfortable with the way that she looked at him on the rare occasion that they were together. Although much of that was now changing, Sadig knew that how women and men lived alongside one another was changing, especially down in Khartoum where they mixed freely in public. There, he had heard, women walked around with their heads uncovered and sat next to men in university halls and parks and buses. He wondered if Fatima would do the same if she left the village to study in Khartoum. He wondered if he would mind.

Sadig stretched and rolled over onto his side to join the other boys in their chitchat. The second shift of the night had begun and while the village slept on, Sadig and two of his cousins had set up camp by the riverbank, at the spot where the missing boy had last been seen. They lay around a bright kerosene lamp on low, roped beds, their sandals under the thin mattresses, wary of scorpions and insects creeping out of the underbrush. Like everyone else, Sadig knew who Mohamed Hamid Kheir Alseed was. The rich boy with the chipped tooth who occasionally played football with them when there weren't enough 'men' to make the team. He was a nice enough boy who never got in trouble with anyone – mostly because people were terrified of his father – but also because he was not the trouble-making kind. Sadig knew the kind of games children played in the river, having played them himself when he was younger. Like Fatima, he doubted Mohamed and the other boys had been sitting quietly on the bank when a sudden wave had swept them from it. He was sure the boy lay not far from where they were camped, waiting for the river to spit his small body out.

The still, hot air hung around them heavily, pushing against their skin, drawing moisture from their brows and armpits. They were in the middle of the dry season and the Nile was low and lethargic. The boys felt a sense of importance at their assigned task. They knew that even if the body didn't surface on their watch, they were still looked on by the villagers with appreciation and respect.

They took turns to keep watch as the night drew on, one boy sitting by the water while the others slept. Sadig chose to take the second shift, and when the stars had moved to the other side of the sky he was shaken awake by his cousin, Abbas, who promptly dropped onto the cool sheets beside him and immediately fell asleep. Sadig sat by the riverside watching the current reflecting the starlight. He tried to keep his mind both blank and occupied at the same time; to stay awake and sight the body but also to keep his mind from dwelling on things he didn't want to think about. So he began reciting the Quran, starting with the verses he had memorized most recently. This was a relatively new activity for him: aside from the Quranic school teachings of his early childhood, he hadn't spent much time learning the Quran. He had picked up the interest from Abbas, whose limbs hung over the sides of the angareeb behind him. Sadig and Abbas both accompanied the camel convoys north to Egypt where they were sold, and during the long hours spent under the hot sun, rocking side to side on the slow-moving beasts, surrounded by endless desert, Sadig listened to Abbas reciting endless streams of Quranic verses in a low, musical voice. At first, he had paid little attention, focusing instead on the stories and laughter from the front of the convoy, where the older men recalled past journeys and shared dirty stories, both memories and those made up during the solitary trail north. But eventually, he found himself drawn closer to Abbas's humming recitation. He wondered at how easily it came to his cousin, how he could recall so much and unfurl it from his tongue without a hitch or mistake.

'It's easy, you should try it yourself. Just listen closely. Understand the words, purify your intentions and open your heart, and you'll find the words rolling off your tongue with no difficulty.'

'That's easy for you to say,' Sadig had complained. 'You're the most intelligent boy in the group and you memorise anything you hear from the first time. I'm nothing like that.'

But he tried: he purified his intentions and listened to the words with an open heart. And sure enough, though not from the first or second try, he picked up where he had left off all those years ago and kept going. On their last trip north, Abbas and Sadig had taken turns reciting and correcting each other, Sadig's reading hitching and full of mistakes at first but smoothing out eventually, until he could almost match Abbas's harmonious voice. It was the most enjoyable journey either of them had taken.

Sadig stopped reading abruptly and turned around. He thought he had heard a sound coming from the trees behind them. He peered into the darkness but couldn't see anything. Then he heard it again and stood up, his pulse quickening. There was someone, or something, moving around there.

He heard a cough and then a man emerged from the gardens and stepped out onto the flat earth. Sadig's heart rate returned to normal.

'Babikir,' he sighed, as the man's round, perspiring face shone under the low light.

'Sadig, I didn't mean to startle you,' Babikir said. He lowered the sack he was carrying over his shoulder to the ground and coughed again, thumping his chest. Babikir Sidahmed was notorious for his smoking habit and always smelled of cigarettes, like he did now. No one knew how he could afford them or where he found them with all the shortages. He coughed again and spat a large plug of phlegm out onto the ground. The two other boys slept on, oblivious.

'No luck yet, I see.'

'Nothing yet. But I doubt the body will float tonight. It's too early.'

'Aye,' Babikir said, stepping close to the riverside and peering down into the water. He was careful not to lean too far over so that his expansive belly wouldn't shift his balance and cause him to topple. 'It is too early, but with children you can never be too sure. Wad Alsafi's daughter floated on the same night. I remember like it was yesterday.'

Many years ago, there had been three Wad Alsafi girls. Now there were two.

'What are you doing up so early? Fajr prayers are still hours away.'

Babikir Sidahmed straightened up and stretched his back, yawning widely as if the mention of the time had reminded him of how tired he was.

'Dropping off the grain for the camels before I catch the early bus to Tangasi. I'll need to pray Fajr there if I'm going to make it to the camel auctions in time. We had a good year and I'm looking to expand my herd.'

'That's good news. More camels for our journey north, then.'

They talked companionably together in low voices, anticipating the good times ahead whilst mindful of the current circumstance they were in.

Babikir picked back up his sack of grain, threw it over his shoulder, and headed off into the trees.

'Nafisah will be sending down your morning tea at daybreak,' he called back, before disappearing into the palms.

Sadig turned and walked slowly back to his watching post. It was almost time to hand over to Gasim, but he would stay up for a while to finish the Sura he was reading.

Babikir Sidahmed made his way up the winding dirt road toward the herding grounds behind the village. It was still dark with an hour left for Fajr prayers, and another hour and a half until the sun rose. The grain he was carrying would be added to the camels' breakfast of grass and dry dates to keep their blood iron levels up. Babikir didn't want them getting weak blood at this time of the year. Now that gasoline and diesel were unaffordable, there was renewed interest in camels and they were predicted to attract good prices. As the road grew steeper it turned from plain to hill, and he shifted the weight of the heavy sack of grain from one shoulder to the other, panting with the effort. Babikir kept telling himself that he should cut back on cigarettes. He could only afford the low-quality local kind, but even they weren't cheap. His wife regularly reminded him of all the things they could have bought with the money he spent on cigarettes. And that all that smoke was rotting his gut on the inside and one day he would wake up with a hole burnt right through his throat and out the back of his neck. He laughed at her dramatic predictions, but recently he had found himself touching his throat when he woke up and sighing with relief when he found it intact.

Babikir passed by his sister's house and paused near the wall, listening for any sound from within. He knew she would be awake at this time and sure enough he heard running water and ablutions from within. He called out in a low voice:

'Asha?'

'Hababak my brother Babikir,' came her reply. 'Any news of the boy?'

'No, the boys haven't seen anything yet. They –'

He stopped abruptly. Something had moved a short distance ahead of him. He stared into the darkness, trying to make out what or who it was. He was almost sure it had been a person. But there was nothing now.

'Babikir?'

His sister called him from behind the wall.

'Yes, I'm here,' he said, still looking down the road. 'Sorry, I thought I saw someone.'

'At this hour?' she sounded doubtful. 'Probably Al-Abbassi heading out of town. Today's Monday, he would be heading to Al Dabbah for the crop market. Though it is quite early, even for him.'

'Maybe,' Babikir nodded, doubtfully. He couldn't be sure in the dim light.

'What about you? Are you still going to Shendi? It will be difficult for you to go all that way and come back before nightfall.'

'I'll head out as soon as I've checked on the camels. I've already got my bus ticket. Mahdi Taha will pick me up near the mosque in less than an hour. I'll be back after tomorrow by sunset in sha'Allah.'

'Belsalama in sha' Allah, stay safe.'

Babikir re-shouldered his sack of grain and continued up the road, peering into the alleys and side streets along the way for anyone else up and about. It was probably one of the village boys roaming around on some midnight adventure. Their village was a small one. Everyone knew everyone, and they were all related in one way or another. That made it difficult for mischief to be done, because everyone would know about it and the embarrassment would chase the family for generations.

Of course, occasionally, things did happen.

Everyone remembered how a stray bullet shot during Seif Eldin Homri's wedding celebration nineteen years ago had killed Babikir's nephew, and still gossiped about how the Satti boy had been drunk when he stabbed Bakri Hamad's youngest daughter after she had turned down his marriage proposal. There were always rumours, often around deaths. No, Babikir wasn't scared of what was moving around in the shadows. What made him uncomfortable was that he was almost sure it had been a woman.

There was something else that was strange, Babikir thought, as he stood in front of his camel pen, his heart pumping loudly and his breath raspy. It was almost completely quiet in the camel pen. He owned a modest herd of eight camels and three calves, and they knew their feeding times. They usually greeted him from afar with roars of hunger, demanding their breakfast, their long necks reaching over the pen walls as soon as he passed the last line of houses. But today there was nothing. No bobbing heads, no neighing, no impatient snorts. Had the camels been stolen? That wasn't unheard of, even in their small village. The pen was a distance from the houses and he did not keep it guarded. There were always nomad Arabs loitering around, or those pestiferous gypsies. He took a few more steps before he heard the camels: laboured, choppy breathing; wheezing.

He looked over the pen wall and dropped the sack of grain to the ground, its contents pouring out unceremoniously into the sand.

The camels were there alright, no animals were missing. But the adult camels were lying on the ground paralysed in strange, contorted positions. Some had small pools of blood near their mouths, and white froth around the nostrils. They were all motionless. They were not breathing, except for one of the females at the back, who was lying on her side, her breathing cracked and painful, with her two calves standing near her head. The calves seemed unfazed. They were standing next to their mothers in a calm silence. The wheezing stopped.

It took several minutes for Babikir to comprehend what he was looking at. When his brain finally registered that his entire herd – save the calves – was dead, he stepped quietly back from the gate. His brain grinded slowly against the inside of his skull, trying to compute what he was seeing with what he knew. He had been around animals long enough to know that if something could kill an entire herd overnight it must be highly contagious and could potentially infect humans as well. He had never seen something like this before. Was it a bleeding fever? Like what animals smuggled in from west Africa brought with them? They had had two outbreaks of that before and while they devastated the livestock, the animals had died in crops over several days. And there had been a lot of blood. This wasn't like that. There was only a little blood, and these camels had all died within a few hours. He knew that because he had been with them right after sunset prayers, delivering their dinner and filling the water tubs from the water channel.

His eyes still on the dead animals, Babikir backed further away from the pen. The sack of grain lay forgotten against the wall, its fallen contents scattered by the pre-dawn breeze. Inside, the calves shifted around, looking down at their mothers and waiting for them to stand up and feed them. But their mothers lay silently in the sand, their eyes wide open in surprise or in pain – it wasn't clear which. Babikir turned around and retraced his steps down the sand dunes towards the village. Some disconnected thoughts drifted around in his head. The first was a furtive calculation of how much damage this had done to him. His income almost exactly equalled his expenditure, and he was always just a few pounds above the water. Babikir's camels were the single largest source of income for him: he used them for transport, rented them out to carry the full sacks and equipment during the date harvest season, and their milk was a prized source of nutrition and healing for the villagers. When it was absolutely necessary, a fully-grown adult sold for almost five hundred pounds, and that kept him and his family going for many months.

The second thought that slowly seeped into Babikir's head as he shuffled unsteadily home under a dawn sky was how had this happened to him? No, *why* had this happened? To him? Had the camels been poisoned? He didn't have any enemies that he knew of and he didn't know what poison and in what vast quantity could kill not just one adult camel, but eight of them. But if it wasn't poison, he thought, then what else could it be?

Babikir came to a slow stop at a cross-roads. His mind flitted back to the shadow, his eyes drawn west towards the far end of the village, to where the houses became more and more dilapidated, to the open land where the rootless nomads and Gypsies set up camp during the date harvest season under the low rocky hills where nothing good grew.

Maybe it wasn't poison, Babikir Sidahmed thought, but witchcraft.

Five

That morning, the villagers woke up to the discovery that every adult camel, sheep or goat on the west side of the village was either dead or dying. The news was so devastating that even the missing boy was forgotten. By the time the sun had reached the middle of the sky the official count was 325 animals. The only animals that had not died were the goats most villagers kept in small pens inside their homes for their milk, the horses and cows that pulled the sawagi that hauled up water in the date gardens, and the donkeys that pulled the carts in the village marketplace.

'It's the bleeding sickness, it has to be,' one man said as he stood with a group of villagers looking over a small pen covered with dead goats. The owner, Zamzam, was a widow and mother of five children. She sat on her haunches a short distance away from them, wailing loudly and rocking back and forth. The stack of berseem that she had harvested from her small plot and brought to feed her animals lay discarded beside her.

'Have patience, woman!' Sheikh Abdallah, the village imam told Zamzam. 'This is a test from Allah! Have patience and don't complain about your fate!'

'We've seen what the bleeding sickness does to animals and this isn't what it looks like,' Mohamed Altahir said doubtfully. He leaned over the low fence to get a better look at the goat closest to him. 'Last time it hit us, Abdalgadir Ehmoudi lost his animals over two weeks. What could kill all these animals together this quickly?'

'This is a test from Allah and we must have patience.'

'Yes, yes we know that,' another man said, 'but what caused it? We need to know! What if it's something in the soil or the water that could infect humans as well? What if it infects the chickens and pigeons? What about the trees and wheat? Our village will be ruined!'

'We should pray to Allah that this doesn't go any further and to forgive whatever sins we have committed that caused this to befall us.'

The men clicked their tongues, folded their hands behind their backs and turned to inspect the damage further down the road, leaving the sobbing woman behind them to pull up fists full of dirt and smear it over her head. Inquiries were made in the surrounding villages. Whatever had inflicted their livestock had not touched any of the neighbours. The villagers recounted the last bleeding sickness again: the entire region had been affected by it, albeit in a patchy manner. But it was still too early to tell. The discovery was only a few hours old.

That afternoon a phone call was made from the imam's house to the regional veterinary office in Dongola, describing what had befallen the animals, the numbers, the fact that only the adults had been affected. Would a veterinarian be dispatched, and discretion kept? News like this would be particularly devastating as not only were the livestock a staple source of income, but also the dates and citrus fruits from their village might be assumed to be poisoned, and the villagers would lose the market for those as well. The veterinary office promised it would send someone to take samples, but that it would take some time. And someone did leave the office that same afternoon, but the car he was driving punctured its tyre only a few kilometres from the office and the spare was flat.

The villagers were on their own for now.

❧

Fatima stood near the small Primus stove waiting for the tea to boil so that she could pour it into the small tea pot with its mint leaves. She kept one eye on the water and the other on the open door that led into the back alley and from there to the men's deiwan and yard. The kitchen was a small, narrow room. A cement counter lined the wall opposite the door, with large, open cupboards underneath it. Stacked on the ground in a small space between the wall and the end of the counter were the food trays and the large, shallow steel tub in which the dishes were washed, and on the other side by the door leading to the ally was a large barrel of water. The Primus stove was perched in the middle of the counter, the spices to its right and a breadbasket to its left. On the adjacent wall were two tall cupboards with net-covered doors where the regular glasses and dishes were stored; the fancier dishes and cutlery were kept in Habiba's room and brought out only for important guests and special occasions. Opposite the counter behind the door was the roped bed on which the dishes were put to dry, and in the corner was the large standing oven that Habiba turned on several times a month to make bread, gargosh, and different types of cookies depending on the occasion. Just yesterday she and a group of other women had finally finished baking the cookies for Sawsan's wedding, which were stored in buckets and would be covered in powdered sugar on the morning of the wedding. The main kitchen door led in from the verandah, and a smaller door led out of the kitchen and into the narrow alley that wrapped around the back of the house, where they hung the washing.

Her father's voice travelled through the warm afternoon air down the alley and into the kitchen and Fatima eavesdropped intently, trying to catch every word. Her mother was straightening the bedsheets on the beds in the front yard, as she had been doing for quite a while. Fatima knew she was eavesdropping as well.

'Who do we collect money for and who do we leave? This is a catastrophe.'

'It must have been something in the soil. Whenever seasons change strange things come out of the ground and sometimes they can poison the earth. How do we know this won't affect the people as well?'

'But the seasons changed several weeks ago,' Fatima heard her father say as she turned off the stove, picked up the steel kettle with the folded edge of her scarf and poured the tea into the pot. There were six small glasses on the tray and her mother's good sugar bowl with two small teaspoons. Fatima took her time arranging the glasses and wiping away some of the sugar that had spilled on the counter.

'Whatever it is, we have a pretty good idea who and what is most likely behind it,' she heard Eltayeb Salim growl. He was her father's cousin and had lost thirteen goats that morning, but unlike the widow and many other villagers, he had two large plots of land with mango trees which would

46

provide some buffer against the devastating loss. 'Babikir said he saw someone lurking around in the dark last night. A woman.'

'Let's not jump to any conclusions.'

'Oh, spare me your intellectual nonsense. This is no simple infection that killed all these animals. Someone either poisoned them or let loose a powerful djinn to do this scale of damage.' Fatima heard murmurs of assent. Then her uncle – and future father-in-law – Haj Mutasim spoke up.

'The question isn't what person could be powerful enough to carry out this damage, but why? What motive would anyone have to inflict such disaster on our village? We don't even know who this person might be or where they have come from.'

The rest was inaudible. Either the men had stopped talking or had lowered their voices further. Fatima glanced through the open door at her mother to see her standing still in the front yard, a pillowcase in her hand, straining to hear as well. They both jumped when her father's voice cracked across the alley:

'Fatima! Bring the tea!'

Fatima threw the cleaning cloth onto the countertop and quickly picked up the tray, hurried down the steps and into the alleyway, around the back of the house and entered the men's yard. Her father didn't look at her as she pulled out a small metal side table, placed it between the two beds the men were sitting on, and put the tray on it. Aside from her father and uncles there was Abdelhakeem, another cousin of her father's, their next-door neighbour, Tijani Sidahmed, and his brother, Babikir Sidahmed – the camel herder who had raised the alarm early that morning.

Fatima started to pour spoonfuls of sugar into the glasses, but her father sat forward, took the spoon from her hands, and dismissed her. They waited until she had left before starting to talk again in low voices that were inaudible from the kitchen. Fatima stood by the door for a short while straining to hear but gave up eventually. Exasperated, she stepped back into the kitchen, wiped the counter and put tea things away. Then she covered her mouth to stifle a giggle.

It was always funny to her how her father kept up the pretence of gruffness towards her in the presence of others, particularly the men in her extended family. He would put on a serious expression, look the other way when she spoke and dismiss her as soon as possible. When Khalid was still alive she would have to call him to pick up the tray or deliver a message when there were guests over. But when they were alone, it was a different story. They used to play cards and Ludo and take turns imitating people and guessing who it was. Though not an avid reader himself, Mohamed Altahir would share interesting bits he found in the newspapers he brought home and gave Fatima a regular allowance to save up for the small story books she and some of the neighbourhood children read: *Rajol Almustaheel, Almughamiroun Alkhamsa, Ma Wara' Altabe'a*. They didn't have a bookstore in their small village, so Fatima gave her monthly savings to Fathiya bit Zainab who gave it to her husband Haj Adam on his bimonthly trip to Karima where he would purchase the newest titles for her.

But as with everything else in their lives, Fatima's relationship with her father had changed after Khalid's death. He still read bits of the newspaper out loud as he lay on his back in the yard, sipping tea. And he listened to

Fatima's summaries of the latest story she had read, asking the right questions to show that he was following along. But there were no more games, no more funny imitations. She was also older now and that created an even bigger distance between them as she approached womanhood and would soon move into another man's house.

Fatima stepped out of the kitchen, crossed the verandah and out into the yard, turning towards the back of the house. She heard the goat bleating in its small shed to her right and stepped over the scrawny chicks scrounging around behind their mother as she entered the shade of the other kitchen. A mountain of onions greeted her. She needed to finish her chores early so that she could make it to Sawsan's house before the unwelcome cousins arrived. Fatima sunk down onto the low rope bed with a sigh, feeling sorry for herself.

Not much cooking was actually done inside; the Primus stove in the smaller kitchen was used only for making tea and coffee, heating milk or fava beans, or sometimes frying eggs for a quick breakfast or supper. The bulk of the cooking was done in the other kitchen – the tukul – in the far corner of the house. This was an open walled room with a packed dirt floor and date fronds for a roof. In the corner was the original cooking area: a low mound of large stones between which dry date fronds and coal were lit and the flat, blackened pan was placed on top for making gurasa. In the other corner was a medium-sized coal burner with a pot on top. Fatima caught a whiff of the fava beans that had been cooking on the low heat since morning. There were different sized coal burners and aluminium cooking pots, stacked from large to small, to the side. A half-full sack of coal leaned against the wall near the door and a low, long table was covered in jars of salt, ground coriander, pepper, chilli powder, fennel and cinnamon, with a large mortar and pestle for pounding the garlic. In the third corner was the stone mortar half buried in the ground which they used to grind wheat and millet. From the roof hung a net with a small pot in it with yesterday's leftovers, kept cool with the breeze coming in from the door and small windows lining the wall. There was also a wire line crossing from one side to the other with strips of dried meat hanging from it. A couple of low roped stools stood near the cooking stations and a low roped bed with uneven legs leaned against the wall.

'Are you going to help Sawsan with her clothes today?'

Habiba came into the tukul and took the other knife. She sat down next to Fatima on the low bed and reached out for an onion.

'Yes, we'll try and get them all perfumed and wrapped this afternoon.'

'Who else is coming?'

'The other Fatima and her sisters.'

'That's nice. It's good that you're all getting together and helping. It will be your turn soon and you'll have lots of help then.'

'Married women become mysteriously unavailable to help with things, I've noticed.'

Habiba laughed.

'Well, you'll find out yourself soon enough how busy marriage makes you.'

Fatima rolled her eyes internally and kept her face carefully averted. She didn't want to offend her mother and knew that her face always betrayed what she was thinking, which right now was how ridiculous all this importance placed on marriage was. It was such a dramatic affair: the preparations, the ceremonies, the expectations and the sudden elevation in social status. When girls were married they suddenly became important and relevant. Not as important as the older women or – God forbid – the men, but still higher up on the food chain than unmarried girls. Fatima pictured herself simmering away in the heat of her own tukul – or actually her in-laws' one since they would be living with Sadig's parents – stirring at the large pots, sweating and blinking from the smoke of the burning branches. She would be wrapped in her jersey tob, her gold bracelets jangling noisily, surrounded by her neighbours who would gather around during the day to drink herbal tea and gossip. Sawsan would be there too, most likely pregnant.

None of this interested her. Fatima wanted to talk about the dead animals. It fascinated her that entire herds could drop dead overnight, and now there were suddenly all these orphaned babies sitting around. She had never thought animals could experience loss, even for the primitive reason that they were now deprived of their main source of nutrition. She also wanted to know what the men were being so secretive about.

'What were they talking about before? About someone being responsible for the dead animals?'

Fatima watched her mother out of the corner of her eye. Habiba hesitated just a little. When she spoke, her voice was slightly high-pitched.

'People say things like this when something happens. You know how superstitious we are.' She laughed, unconvincingly.

'But who were they talking about? Who is this person?'

Habiba acted as if she hadn't heard her and continued with her cutting. She pursed her lips and screwed her eyes closed, trying to keep the onion fumes out of her eyes.

'Is it the same woman they say predicts deaths?'

Habiba stopped, her knife mid onion. Fatima stopped cutting as well and turned to look at her, a little worried. She had been careful to say 'death' instead of 'drowning,' but it was the same thing, and any reference to drowning immediately brought Khalid into the room.

'I... I was just wondering why everyone thinks someone did this.'

Habiba didn't look up at her, and eventually resumed her cutting, though slower than before. She had always been quiet and soft spoken, but she had folded further in on herself in recent years. It seemed nothing much interested her anymore, nothing held her attention for long. Khalid hadn't been the only child she – they – had lost. There had been other children: a boy before Khalid, two girls between Khalid and Fatima, and two boys in the end. Fatima remembered the youngest one, Omar. He was three years younger than her. She had random memories of him, like when he was taking his first steps and had approached Tijani Sidahmed's cat who sometimes jumped over the wall and into their yard to watch the chickens. The cat had ignored him at first, and simply swished her tail away from his pudgy probing fingers. But when he tripped and fell right on top of her, she had flashed around and scratched him across the face.

When he was almost three, Omar had developed a fever along with several other children in the neighbourhood. Fatima remembered her parents' distress even though she didn't fully understand what was happening. Then she was left in Sawsan's house for several fun-filled days while her parents travelled to Karima to take Omar to see the Chinese doctors. They came back without him.

Children died all the time in their area; it was one of the reasons why women gave birth so frequently, since they would lose many of them. They died of febrile illnesses, diarrhoea, wasting, almost all before they turned five years old. So when a child escaped death in their early years and lived long enough to see their teens it was a celebration of life, a feeling of triumph, a blessing to be thankful for every day. And when death caught up with them in those later years, it was a hundred times more painful.

But it wasn't just that. Habiba wasn't like the other village women, thriving on gossip and backbiting and superstitions. Even though she had no formal education after the few years of Quranic school where she learned basic literacy and maths, she read everything she could get her hands on, which wasn't a lot, in their area. Fatima sometimes wondered what her mother would have accomplished if she had finished her education. With her level-headed thinking she stood out from the other women in the family and in the village. Fatima thought she could have been a doctor.

'It's just superstition,' she said in a low voice just as Fatima was giving up on the conversation. 'They believe a soothsayer used to ambush people in the village streets, who she cursed with death by drowning.'

It was Fatima's turn to stop cutting now. She had heard a version of this story several times, a long time ago, but had thought it was one of those stories that adults told children to scare them into coming home before dark.

'Is this woman, this *soothsayer*, a real person? Has anyone actually seen her?'

Habiba let the silence fill the space between them as she organised her thoughts.

'People have seen her,' she said shortly. Fatima waited.

'And? Do her prophecies come true?'

'I don't know, Fatima,' she sighed and put her knife down. 'They say that anyone who sees her drowns eventually. But it's not as if drowning requires a prophecy around here.'

She got up and Fatima knew that the discussion was over. She didn't want to push the matter any further anyway, not just because of the effect it had on her mother, but because it bothered her as well. A strange woman roaming around in the dark and cursing people? Fatima hurried through the remaining onions and covered the pot in which she had put them. Grabbing the short broom and steel shovel leaning on the wall she swept up the discarded peels, stuffed them in the waste bucket in the corner and dashed into the bathroom for a quick wash to get rid of the smell. As she scooped up water from the bucket and splashed it over her, she stared up at the low ceiling and mulled over what her mother had told her – but also what she hadn't. The bathroom was small and bare: a square cement hut with a low ridge along the wall on which they put their bars of soap and loofas, a small window near the ceiling to let in the light, and a hole at the bottom of the wall through which the water drained out and into the garden. There were cobwebs in the corner near the roof, hosting several different sized spiders with long, spindly legs. This was the women's bathroom, adjacent to the small outhouse that opened in the other direction. The men's section had its own bathroom on the other side of the house.

When Fatima emerged from her room a while later dressed up and ready to go, she heard voices from the kitchen and popped her head in to see who her mother was talking with. It was Nasima, one of the Kheir Alseed's servants who dropped in to see Habiba every now and then and always brought with her a wealth of gossip. Even though Fatima was late she still loitered around after greeting Nasima, wanting to hear the latest updates.

'It's terrible,' Nasima said as she sat on the small bed in the tukul, sipping her red tea. On the ground next to her feet was a half empty cloth bag. She had been out to get bread from the bakery and some carrots and onions, but there was a shortage everywhere because everyone was busy with the business of the dead animals.

'I stood in line for half an hour at Alfatih's bakery, as if I was in Khartoum! And when I got to the window he only gave me ten pieces of bread. Ten! For the Kheir Alseed household! That boy must be out of his mind.'

Hearing Nasima talk was always entertaining for Fatima, not just because of the outrageous things she said and the way she described them, but because of her strange Arabic: a mix of Nilotic mispronunciations and the drawl of the Northern state's accent. Even as she sat on the low bed she still towered over them. Nasima was one of a set of families who served in the Kheir Alseed household and a few others, women and men from South and West Sudan who had been in the area for generations. Their grandparents had been enslaved and brought to the north years before, and when slavery had been outlawed in the early 1900s they had been freed but remained in the service of those households.

Nasima gave them an updated list of which villagers had lost how many animals, along with a rough calculation of how much it would cost them and how much worse off they would now be. However, when Habiba questioned her about the Kheir Alseed livestock, she became faithfully evasive.

'Well, you know, they're divided among so many different pens and lots it would be difficult to know the damage so soon.'

Fatima snorted but Nasima ignored her. She sipped the rest of her tea while dispatching fragments of news here and there, and then mentioned that she needed to pass by Khadija's house to help with her daughter Sawsan's wedding preparations. Fatima slapped her forehead and threw a hasty goodbye to Nasima and rushed out of the kitchen.

A few minutes later she was walking hastily down the street towards her cousin's house, already late. Sawsan would be pouting. Fatima had already upset one person today and didn't want to do the same to another.

'You're late,' Sawsan whined as Fatima tumbled into her room.

'I had to cut a thousand onions for lunch. Not all of us are brides-to-be and exempt from kitchen duties.'

'Well, let's get on with it then!'

The room smelled spectacular. Sawsan was standing in the middle of piles of clothing, bags and footwear. On the floor lined against the wall were large glass decanters of scented oils, dilka and khumra; traditional Sudanese perfumes made with a mixture of sandaliya, musk, spices and French scents. Only married women used these perfumes. The groom's family bought the ingredients as part of the dowry and the older, experienced women prepared the perfumes and frankincense in a small ceremony. Sawsan's mother would give out small bundles of the frankincense to the other village women as gifts. A bride getting her own set of perfumes was an important rite of passage that all young girls dreamed about, except maybe Fatima.

A tall incense burner was perched on the windowsill and large clumps of burning coal glowed from within. As part of the wedding preparations, the bride's new clothing sets would be perfumed with musk and sandalwood incense, folded neatly and wrapped up, each set of matching tob, sandals and bag together. These would be shown off to visiting women later, before they would be packed into the suitcases for Sawsan to take to her matrimonial home.

'Hand me that small bag over there. Let's put these three in. What do you think of this one?'

Sawsan held up a pale blue tob with purple and turquoise embroidery.

'It's beautiful,' Fatima said.

'Then in it goes.'

'Honestly,' Fatima laughed as she stuffed the tobs into the bag, 'are you really going to hide all the beautiful pieces so that your cousins don't give them the evil eye and burn holes into them?'

'It's not funny, Fatima,' Sawsan huffed as she rummaged through the pile next to her looking for one tob in particular. 'You know what they're like. They jinx everything they look at and I'm not taking any risks.'

She pulled out a bright orange tob from the pile and handed it to Fatima.

'I don't know how you believe all this stuff. It's all –'

'Just put them in so we can hide the bag! I don't need your nonsense-talk now!'

Fatima took the tob and crammed it into the bag, just as someone knocked on the front door. They heard Sawsan's mother greeting the callers and a chorus of voices reply.

'They're here!' Sawsan hissed in panic, grabbing things at random and throwing them to Fatima.

'Where do I put the bag?'

'Just stick it under the bed!'

Fatima kicked the lumpy bag and the last two tobs Sawsan had thrown at her under the bed as the bedroom door opened and four girls trooped in.

'Sawsan! Just look at you, you're positively glowing.'

Fatima – the other Fatima – stepped forward to embrace her cousin, smelling deeply, her eyes roaming hungrily all around the room, taking note of each item. Her smile stopped short of her sharp eyes which, when they alighted on Fatima, looked her dramatically up and down in an adolescent show of dislike. She let Sawsan go and reached her hand out to Fatima in cold greeting. There was no love lost between the two. The other Fatima and Sawsan's fathers were cousins, while Sawsan and Fatima's mothers were sisters. All of them were related to each other in some way but still separated into different camps.

Fatima returned the up-and-down look with a small sneer as Sawsan embraced the younger sisters and cousin who had tagged along. They picked up bits of clothing and accessories, ooh-ing and aah-ing, admiring Sawsan's good luck and parading their envy. The groom's family picked and bought all the items along with lengths of material that would be sewn into dresses to match the tobs, each set of clothing complete with a pair of matching sandals and handbag. It was a matter of luck – or the lack of it – for the bride depending on her in-laws' good or hideous taste.

'This colour is all the rage now. You'll be just as dashing as the girls in Khartoum!'

Sawsan laughed nervously, pulling the garment out of the other Fatima's hands and folding it tightly away. Fatima contained her mirth as well as she could. Perfuming the bride's clothes was an important and happy occasion, and she didn't want to ruin the day for Sawsan. Whenever the two Fatimas were together in the same room there was almost always a showdown for one reason or another; Fatima just couldn't stand the other's stupidity and insatiable appetite for gossip and backbiting. The other Fatima thrived on talking trash about anyone and everyone, half of which she made up, and a sizeable proportion of which was about Fatima herself.

They divided the work among them. Sawsan brought out the large glass jars of sandalwood incense from under the bed. She put a few sugary sticks over the coals and handed it to the other Fatima who positioned herself on a low stool on the ground, breathing in with relish the perfumed smoke as it bloomed. Outside, the house bustled with movement and the front door opened and shut more than once as other women came to help Sawsan's mother with the wedding preparations such as grounding the spices, prepping vegetables and meat, cleaning out the storerooms and wrapping the gifts for the groom's family. There were four days left until the wedding and these were the busiest days of all. However, what would have usually been a festive atmosphere with laughter, ululations, fits of singing and dancing was relatively subdued as the early events of the day overshadowed them.

Tomorrow, Sawsan would begin the preparations for the wedding ceremony, including sugar waxing followed by the bridal henna that would cover her hands, forearms, feet and shins. Fatima and the other girls would also have some henna drawn, but only one hand as they were still unmarried. She wondered – and she suspected Sawsan did too – whether these preparations would go ahead as planned with the sad events of today and yesterday. Especially if Sulafa's son was found, meaning there would be mourning. Usually, when there was a death in the village weddings were either postponed completely or went on without obvious celebration. Out of courtesy the wedding family would inform those in mourning that they would postpone or cancel their celebrations, and the latter would usually insist things go as planned. Would that happen now?

'So, what do you think of Sulafa's boy going missing? Do you think they'll find him alive?'

The other Fatima spread a dress out over the coals in the incense burner, keeping it at a dangerously low height as Sawsan watched with terror from the other side of the room.

'When have they ever found someone alive in the river?' Fatima asked with irritation. She despised the sensational tone with which the other Fatima talked about it, as if she was sharing another juicy morsel of gossip. Her mind flashed back to the image of Sulafa that morning, crumpled and weeping.

'Ummi said her friends' neighbour went missing once and they found her alive after four days,' one of the younger sisters piped up. She was tasked with the folding and was doing a terrible job. 'She said they found her all the way in Abu Hamad holding onto a tree branch.'

'She floated *upstream* for four days all the way to Abu Hamad?' Fatima snorted.

'Abu Hamad isn't upstream, its north of here,' the other Fatima retorted.

Fatima rolled her eyes and opened her mouth to reply but caught Sawsan's eye. *Drop it*, the look said. Fatima couldn't be bothered anyway, and knew that what she would have said would be too complicated for the girls to understand. The Nile river was unique not only in that it was the longest river in the African continent and flowed from south to north, but also in that it actually changed course at one point near Abu Hamad so that it flowed in the opposite southwest direction before turning back north at Al Dabbah. So even though Abu Hamad was north of their village, the river couldn't have carried this fictional neighbour in that direction unless she had been swimming with all her might against the current.

Fatima sprinkled white musk over the emerald-green silk which she folded and laid out carefully. She picked up the heavy coal iron, blew on it and pressed gently over the cloth, pressing the perfume in and smoothing out the wrinkles.

'I bet he was cursed by the witch in the mountains.'

Not this nonsense again. Fatima looked up at Sawsan who had stopped her folding and was watching the other Fatima with worry. The younger girls looked eagerly at her too and, enjoying the attention, the other Fatima continued.

'The old lady who lives in the mountains and comes down to the village every few years to curse people. Anyone who sees her and looks her in the eye dies of drowning. They say that she looks at you and whispers "moya", and then it's just a matter of time until you find yourself at the bottom of the river!'

'Ahmed Sharif saw her!' the cousin ventured, referring to her older brother.

'That's strange, I saw him last week at the co-op store and he looked quite alive to me,' Fatima said.

'He saw her,' she insisted, 'but he said as soon as she came down the street towards him he turned and fled as if Iblees's dogs were after him.'

'Thank God he ran, Allah saw him!'

'Yes, thank God otherwise there would be no one to marry you, Fatima!'

The other Fatima gasped dramatically and dropped the tob she was carrying. Sawsan dove just in time to keep it from falling on the burning coal.

'What did you say?'

'Oh stop it, both of you!' Sawsan implored.

'You better tell your cousin to watch her mouth!'

'Or else what? What are you going to do, sit on me?' Fatima said. The other Fatima was voluptuous, her body shape surprisingly mature for her age. While this was generally considered an attractive feature, Fatima found it grotesque.

'This is all superstitious rubbish,' Fatima said, looking at Sawsan pointedly. 'It's just a stupid story people tell to scare little children.'

'Ahmed Shareef saw her! He saw her!'

Sawsan looked upset as she looked from girl to girl, then turned to Fatima. Her eyes flew open and her the colour drained out of her face. The bright red dress she had been folding fell out of her limp hands.

'Fatima!'

Fatima turned away from the girls and looked at Sawsan, intent on defending herself, but Sawsan was not looking at her. She was looking at Fatima's hands. Fatima looked down and cried out in alarm just as the smell of burning fabric reached her nose.

She had burnt a hole with the iron all the way through the silk and down into the blanket underneath.

Six

Sulafa was in a dark place. A place with no air, no light, and no way out. She felt like she was being smothered and no matter where she turned her head there was no relief. She could hear voices around her but from a great distance. She had no idea what was going on in the village with the animals. Her skin was numb, her limbs rubbery and flaccid. Her mouth and throat were dry, her heavy tongue like a thick piece of carpet stuck in place. Two heavy stones were pressing against her temples, grinding their way into her head, threatening to fracture her skull and crush her foggy brain. There was a horrible, wrenching pain in her gut which wouldn't let go, and an endless feeling of falling, falling.

She should never have left Mohamed behind. She had never left him behind before, and this time should have been no different, but Hamid wouldn't let her take him. He had told her to either leave him and go or forget about going at all. The boy was a boy no more, he was a man, and men didn't follow their mothers around everywhere. And she had chosen to go and leave him behind. But she wasn't leaving him behind, she had told herself: she was leaving him with his father, aunts, grandmother. With his family who would take care of him for the two days that she was gone.

'What kind of a man tags along after his mother everywhere holding onto the corner of her tob?' Hamid had been scornful.

But he wasn't a man; he was a child. Her child. Her only child. And she had chosen to leave him and go to that ridiculous wedding, and now she just couldn't understand why she had done such a thing. It was her distant cousin's wedding, not something that was terribly important. She didn't have to go. She went because she wanted to go; to get the hell away from these people and this prison even if just for a couple of days.

As Sulafa lay in the dark, she kept replaying the moment she had decided to go and leave her son behind. She kept replaying it and stopping right before the moment she had made her decision. Replaying and stopping, replaying and stopping. Changing the ending and saying the words: I'm not going. I'll stay here. And everything would have been fine.

But the more she replayed it in her head, the harder it was to stop in time to change the ending, and instead what was repeated in her head was: I'll leave him with his father, it's only two days. And the deeper the darkness became, the harder it was to breathe, the stronger the pain in her gut, the sharper the pain in her head. She couldn't go back and change anything: her son – her only son – was missing in the river. Drowned. Dead. Gone, forever, leaving her just as she had been before he had been born.

Childless and alone.

Sulafa was a motherless child. Her mother had died when she was two years old during the birth of her younger sister, leaving their father with four daughters and two sons under the age of thirteen. She sometimes wondered whether it was her or her newborn sister who was most unfortunate in this loss, and decided that she was, because even though she had no memory of it, she had had a mother for two whole years. Which meant that – despite the fact that she had no memory of it – she had experienced a mother's love before losing it, as opposed to her younger sister who had never experienced it at all, and so had lost nothing. There was always an aunt or distance relative around to 'help with the children', and the newborn baby girl was breastfed by several nursing mothers in the neighbourhood, and so the void left by the dead mother was rapidly covered, but not filled.

Before the newborn baby was three months old, they already had a young, beautiful stepmother living in their mother's quarters. Though not an evil one, she wasn't the warmest hearted, and when her own children were born one after the other, Sulafa and her siblings were gradually pushed into the background: fed, clothed, but unloved. They were not introduced to the guests unless they happened to be in the room, were always referred to as their dead mother's children as opposed to their father's and were not called for or missed when absent from the lunch tray.

Sulafa's mother had come from old money, from a powerful family with several branches spread out over the region. Her father had descended from a long line of Sufi sheikhs who were known far and wide, and to whom people travelled from far off places in search of blessings, treatment, counselling and education. He had lived a modest life with few worldly possessions. He spent his days and early evenings in the Quranic school attached to their house, from where Sulafa and the rest of the family could hear the droning recitals of the students from the early morning. When Sulafa was still a young girl, she sat by her father most of the day as he taught the boys the alphabet, how to read, the tajweed guidelines, and listened to and corrected their Quraan recitation. He reviewed their writing which they did on hard wooden slabs – alwah – with thin sharpened canes dipped in ink, which were washed clean when they were full to write on again. That was how Sulafa learned to read and write. She had memorised the whole Quraan at the age of seven.

As the death of a parent either brings families together or breaks them apart, their motherless family eventually drifted away from each other, each sibling searching for their worth in a family of their own. Their stepmother ushered this process along by helping to secure marriage proposals from good families who were conveniently from villages far from theirs, across the river, and who were attracted by the good names from which the orphans descended. One by one the siblings were dispersed into the world to become spouses and parents and attempt to give the love they had grown up without.

By the time Sulafa turned sixteen, her stepmother – Asha Sidahmed Elnour – and her children had full run of the house, and the remaining orphans were rendered almost invisible. Their father was consumed with his teaching and followers and beseechers, and as the girls grew older, they were no longer a man's business to raise. Despite their personal wealth, they were worthless, floating around unattached to anything or anyone, not belonging anywhere and living like unwanted guests in their own home. And so it was with great joy and relief that Sulafa welcomed the news of her prestigious suitor, Hamid Hassan Kheir Alseed, who came from a village three days travel from her own.

'He's unmarried, young, rich and his family practically owns half their village.'

Asha Sidahmed counted the attractive traits of the suitor, whose interest had been secured through a well-known matchmaker.

'Alawia Hashim only works with high class families and all her matches are a success. You should be happy.'

Sulafa was more than happy. She sometimes wondered why no one had proposed to her until that age, with the abundance of male relatives and there being no shortage of families who wished to develop family ties with her father the Sheikh. Later, she would come to realise that her stepmother acted as gatekeeper to marriage proposals and firmly turned away anyone who did not live far enough away. Hamid Kheir Alseed – encouraged by the matchmaker and her team – had brought more money, gold and gifts than any of her sisters' suitors had. The wedding preparations couldn't pass fast enough for Sulafa and she counted down the days until she would leave her loveless house – hopefully forever.

She was a very beautiful bride by all standards. She wore her late mother's embroidered red jirtik tob on the wedding day, drawing words of admiration and pity from the attendees for her and her siblings' early orphanhood, and comparisons between her and her mother.

'She looks just like her.'

'She looks nothing like her.'

'Asha and Alawia did a good job with this match. Sulafa should thank her lucky stars and kiss her hand back and front.'

'Where are the groom's family from again?'

'From a village somewhere near Alkarafab, or Karima, or somewhere around there. I've never heard of it before, but they're Shaygiya of course. Or Bideriya.'

'Well, they look respectable. Just look at all that gold her mother-in-law has. She looks like a kind person. And the groom, ma sha' Allah, mmmm-mmm! So handsome! They'll take good care of Sulafa, I'm sure.'

Sent off with ululations, good wishes and perfume but no tears at all, Sulafa was carried with no emotional belongings on the lorry that would take her to her matrimonial home. She looked back only once to the house where she had grown up, and felt nothing at all. Her father had not come to see her off, settling for the congratulation and wishes for a good life that he had endowed on both her and the groom as they sat on the platform. It had been the same with all her siblings, so it was no wonder that none of them had ever returned. At their parting, her stepmother gave her her first and only piece of advice.

'Just give them a son. Then you'll be safe.'

'Safe from what?' Sulafa had asked, but Asha Sidahmed just patted her cheek and sent her on her way.

The lorry had blasted out its musical horn at the outskirts of the village, announcing their arrival three exhausting days later. Somehow, she had managed to maintain her looks despite being covered by a film of dust from their tumultuous ride through the desert. She descended from the lorry on wobbly legs, and waded through the crowd of curious children and adults and onto the awaiting donkey cart which carried her, the groom and their bags up through the streets, where men and women stood outside their homes to greet and congratulate them, and get a good look at this new bride from far away. She saw with glee how their – her – house towered over the others with its huge front gates. There she was welcomed with many days and nights of celebration, and an endless barrage of gifts raining down on her from her in-laws and neighbours and family near and far.

She was charmed by the ease of her life as Hamid's wife. She thanked her luck when their first born – a son – arrived less than one year later. But because she had grown up in a home where love was not in abundance, she didn't know what to expect when the nightmare of childbirth was over and the baby was placed into her arms. Would she know how to love him? Would he love her back? What if neither of them figured out how to do this and it never happened?

All those questions evaporated when she looked into the red, wrinkled face with its dark lips and hairy forehead. Instantly, any doubt of her ability to love this child dissipated. Everything and everyone were reduced to an 'else', other than her and this person in her arms; they became invisible, irrelevant, they did not exist. This person was hers. This person was *her*. He was her first true and only family, an extension of her – no, a part of her whole, a part that made her whole, a part without which she was incomplete. She wondered what kind of a life she had been living before this moment. All the years before his arrival seemed like time spent in waiting, waiting for something to make it meaningful. It was as if all her life she had been a wanderer, and now she was finally home. There were two births on that sunny Sunday afternoon: her son's, and her own.

Now, as she floundered around through the thick, warped gloom, the memory of that day cautiously forged its way through the darkness, coaxing her back into the real world. But she turned away. She didn't want to go back to the real world; she didn't want to be anywhere near it when the people who were waiting for her son's body to float got what they were waiting for, giving silent thanks that they could now get on with their lives.

It was getting late and Fatima would have to leave soon. The room was empty save for her and Sawsan. The excited babble outside had faded to silence; everyone had left in the early afternoon. The business with the dead animals had been weighing on the village all day. Several women who should have visited did not come at all, and some duties remained undone because the person who would usually carry them out had not shown up. They heard Sawsan's mother grumbling about the millet that needed to be ground and the coriander seeds that still weren't cleaned.

'If Zamzam doesn't come tomorrow I don't know what I'll do.'

'Have mercy, Khadija. She just lost her one source of income, and she has all those mouths to feed and no husband to support her.'

'I know, I know. I feel so sorry for her. So much bad

luck! But if she doesn't come tomorrow I'll have to take all these seeds down to the mill and those boys do a terrible job. Also, I would rather she have the money than anyone else.'

'Poor woman.'

Fatima listened to this discussion as she stacked the wrapped sets of clothes carefully and arranged them in the last suitcase. She looked up at the iron sitting on the windowsill next to the incense burner, now cool. The green batch of burnt silk still clung to the bottom of it. Fatima wished she could throttle herself, punch herself in the stomach, scratch her own face. Why couldn't she stay out of trouble just this once? Why did she always have to inflict pain on those around her?

'I wonder when they'll marry her off,' she heard the neighbour saying to Khadija. The voices were coming from further away now, as the women stood by the door, where the juiciest conversations usually occurred.

'Do you think they'll be able to after this? Her husband died such a horrible death, her house fell down in the last rainy season and now all her animals are dead from Allah knows what. She's been left with nothing but a mouth full of salt. I wouldn't be surprised if they believed she was cursed.'

'I wouldn't be surprised either. But of course, it's all written by Allah and we can't complain about what He has in store for us.'

Fatima huffed. Cursed? Can't complain about Allah's will? They and surely everyone else in the village had already passed their judgment on the poor Zamzam and sealed her fate. She would live now under this black label until the end of her days, every event justified by the villagers' superstitious interpretations. Fatima knew Zamzam well; everyone did. Her husband had been a bus driver on the Marawi-Khartoum route. Two years ago, he had lost his way in the desert on the way to the capital. He and his forty-five passengers were only found eight days later. All had died of thirst; a fate that was not unheard of but was greatly feared. He had left Zamzam with five children and a mountain of hate for the lives lost, the responsibility for which was placed squarely on her husband, and which she had inherited. Usually, widows were hurriedly married to their brother-in-law after the death of the husband, and the only reason she had lasted this long was that the only brother-in-law she had was thirteen years younger than her. There were cousins that would fill in, but the families had the inheritance to think of, and were in no rush to distribute it among other families.

Fatima turned to look cautiously at Sawsan, who had her back to her and was fumbling with something in her hands. Sawsan hadn't spoken to her since the incident. She had wailed and cried, bringing all the women rushing into the room to share the calamity, making Fatima wish the earth could open up and swallow her whole. She had only spoken directly to Fatima to say she should just drop everything and leave, but Fatima had insisted she stayed and finished the job. The other Fatima and her troupe had left in laughter.

'Oh Fatima, you must be really jealous of Sawsan. Look at how your evil eye burnt that tob right through!'

Fatima heard a sniff and could see Sawsan's slumped shoulders shaking. She cursed her clumsiness again. She didn't know how she could fix what had happened: she did not have the money to buy Sawsan a new tob instead of the one she had burnt, and it was absolutely unacceptable to replace an item someone had damaged or lost, anyway, though Fatima didn't understand why. She sighed sorrowfully for the hundredth time. It was getting dark outside; she was so late.

'Sawsan,' she ventured. Sawsan did not reply. Instead, she let her crying be heard. Fatima walked over to where she was and, without planning to, hugged her tightly from behind.

'I'm so sorry,' she said for the hundredth time that afternoon.

She felt Sawsan shaking with her sobs and felt guilty tears of her own fill her eyes.

'It doesn't matter,' Sawsan whispered. 'I don't care about the tob or about anything else.'

'We'll find another one, I promise. Kaltoum Wahab is sure to have a similar piece. She just tells everyone she has only one piece of everything so people think they're unique.'

'I said I don't care about the stupid tob!' Sawsan wrenched herself free and turned to face Fatima, her wet eyes puffy and her cheeks red. 'What do I want with a stupid tob! What good would it do me? What good would any of this do me when I'm dead!'

Fatima stared at her for a couple of seconds, then her tears turned to those of anger.

'Sawsan, for the hundredth time, all this nonsense about drowning is garbage.'

'How can you be so sure? Everyone knows about it! Everyone has proof!'

'What kind of proof?' Fatima cried in exasperation.

'I saw her, Fatima! I saw her with my own eyes! And she spoke to me! She looked me square in the eye and said it! She pointed at me and said "moya"!'

Fatima hesitated. This story was not new to her. Sawsan had told her and only her about it many years ago, and after the initial shock had subsided they had laughed about it and moved on. It was only recently that Sawsan had taken the so-called prophecy seriously.

'Sawsan,' Fatima reasoned, 'everyone says this *woman* walks around the village at night. When have you ever left the house after sunset? You can't possibly have met her! You just imaged the whole thing!'

'I'm as good as dead,' Sawsan whispered helplessly and fell to the floor in a weeping heap. Fatima knelt down next to her, holding back an exasperated laugh, and hugged her tight.

'It's not true. None of it is, I promise you. Nothing will happen to you. You'll marry that blockhead Omar and have ten babies and live to be a hundred and forty years old.'

She stroked Sawsan's hair and repeated her promise. The whole thing was ridiculous; Sawsan never even went near the river. There was no way she could drown.

Seven

As sunset approached, the last of the dead animals was hauled into Babikir Sidahmed's camel pen on a donkey cart. Sadig and his cousins stood around the pen with the rest of the men who had come to watch. More than half of them had lost their entire livelihood overnight. Sadig watched Babikir Sidahmed out of the corner of his eye. The man seemed to have aged twenty years in the few hours since they had last met. He was sitting on the ground, his turban draped around his neck. His eyes were shining and looking straight ahead, and he appeared to be mumbling under his breath.

Young boys carried small jerry cans of gasoline into the pen and started sloshing it liberally on the piles of animals. Getting around and between the carcasses was difficult; there were so many of them and of varying sizes. They climbed up on to the wall to pour the gasoline from above, but quickly jumped back down when the brittle mud bricks started to crumble and sway under their weight. Gasoline was a precious commodity, especially in a small village like theirs when the whole country was suffering under the economic hardship that the third democracy had inherited from the Nimeiri regime. The villagers used it only sparingly, to power the generators and to operate the two aging tractors and the single bus that formed the village's transport system.

But this was an extenuating circumstance, and no one was thinking about scarcity.

The imam stood at the front of the crowd overlooking the procedures. He called on his fellow villagers to hold on to their faith in Allah at this trying time and reminded them that to pass this test they must have patience and be thankful for the opportunity to examine their faith.

'Pass this test and you will be rewarded, if not in this life, then in the afterlife,' he called on them. His sermon fell on ears that were only half listening. Grief and shock were the main feeling enveloping the men and their families in the homes behind them. But there were other feelings as well, which were gaining traction and growing. They were angry and suspicious of the real cause behind the livestock's sudden and dramatic deaths. Of the wickedness lying at the foot of the mountains.

The boys jumped over the walls and walked out of the pen, keeping the door open. The wind blew dust against them as the men stood in the vast open land, looking into the pen that had housed the boisterous and noisy camels just one day before. Mohamed Altahir stood next to his cousins and, as the imam lit a match and put it to a dry palm frond, he reached forward and put his hand on Babikir Sidahmed's shoulder, gripping it tightly. The palm frond caught fire easily and the imam didn't need to blow on it as the wind kept it alight. He took a few steps forward into the pen, threw the fire into the pile of shining animals, stepped back and pulled the pen gates shut.

The group took a few steps backwards as the pile of dead animals swiftly caught fire and the flames rose rapidly into the air, lighting the evening sky and raising increasingly black smoke. The smell of roasted flesh was not displeasing, and reminded Sadig of the morning of Eid Al Adha when the slaughtered animals were quartered, cut up, cooked and presented in different meals. There were so many animals of varying sizes that it took quite a while for them all to catch on fire, and as the animals burned, and the flames rose higher, the heat became so intense that it continued to drive the men backwards. But no one left. Dusk turned to a night that was as bright as day. Babikir Sidahmed dropped his face into his hands and howled into the crackling night air.

Down in the village the women in their homes watched the bonfire on the sand dunes with the same mixed feelings as the men in front of it. Many of them wept, many were in disbelief, and all wondered what would happen now that the village had lost one of its main sources of revenue. Habiba and Fatima stood on low stools in the kitchen alleyway looking over the wall and gazing at the bonfire lighting the sky in the distance. Even on the far side of the village, the smell of charred flesh reached them in whiffs and waves, though it was not as nauseating as for those whose houses were closer to the dunes. The evening air also carried the sounds of weeping and wailing from the different houses, and Fatima wondered just how much sadness a single village could handle. Her thoughts turned to Sulafa, whose in-laws owned the largest number of animals in the village, all lost to the mysterious ailment. Was her husband up there with the rest of the men burning the carcasses? Or was he down by the water, waiting for his son's body to float?

The whole horizon seemed to light up with the fire. As the flames rose to the west of the village, the light travelled over the houses until it reached the east where the date gardens flanked the river bank. It was so bright it seemed as if even the date gardens themselves were on fire.

Fatima watched the light over the gardens for a few minutes, then realised with a jolt what was happening. The light over the gardens wasn't a reflection of some sort. It was also a fire. A very large fire, right in the middle of the gardens and not at all related to the bonfire on the sand dunes.

'Ummi! Ummi look there! The gardens are on fire!'

Habiba whipped her head around towards where Fatima was pointing and gasped in horror. Before their eyes they could see tongues of flames rising into the sky and spreading, the sound of crackling dry bush reached their ears. The gardens behind them were ablaze.

'Fire! Fire in the gardens!' they heard Mousa's distant screams traveling down the road between the gardens and the houses as the elderly ground keeper came hobbling out into the open. Suddenly, the faint wails around them turned to a high-fevered pitch as the women in the houses caught sight of the fire much closer to their homes, and all panic broke loose.

Up on the dunes, the men were oblivious to what was happening behind them. They listened to the crackling burning of flesh and the recitations of the imam to ward the evil away from their village, bless what remained, instil faith and patience into the hearts of those who had suffered and forgive whatever sins they had committed to turn Allah's wrath against them.

Sadig stood at the edge of the crowd observing the faces around him. Almost every man in the village was there, which meant no one was keeping watch by the river. It was interesting to him how men showed – or didn't show

— their distress. As Sudanese and particularly as Arabs, openly displaying feelings of fear or grief was considered unacceptably effeminate, a betrayal to their solid and unwavering masculinity. He supposed it was something they had inherited from their warrior ancestors; possibly, showing their emotions would betray their weakness to the enemy. There was a constant need for them to reinforce this image and remind everyone of the clear distinction between them and the women.

'Men don't cry.'

'Men fear nothing.'

'We might as well put scarves on our heads and cower down inside our houses like women.'

From what Sadig could see, upholding an unscathed image of virility was the last thing on several men's minds this evening. Babikir Sidahmed was not the only man openly crying, although his wails were the loudest. Most of the other men kept their eyes averted to spare him any embarrassment. Others, however, stared at him with open disgust, like Hamid Kheir Alseed. He stood at the back of the crowd, the light from the fire dancing across his face, throwing his already hard features into alternating flatness and relief. It amplified his customary look of anger and contorted it into something more: rage, anguish, distress. Sadig couldn't tell. But he could guess that if whatever had happened to them had been caused by a person, then that person should flee for their life before Hamid Kheir Alseed caught hold of them.

Around him, he heard the men whispering among themselves.

'Did you hear what Tijani Sidahmed said?'

'Yeah, I heard. And I tell you, it's not that difficult to believe.'

'All this death, it must have been black magic. This is unnatural.'

'Someone must have a serious score to settle.'

'With us?'

Sadig was wondering about the same thing. Like the others, he had heard of the scary woman who predicted people's deaths. But unlike Fatima, he did not dismiss these stories as fairy tales, nor did he dismiss the theory that a supernatural force had caused the death of all these animals. So why not the same woman? As for the reason she seemed to hate them all so much, he didn't think about for too long. Some people were just evil.

He looked at Hamid Kheir Alseed again, then down at the village behind them which dipped down from the dunes towards the date gardens to the far east and from there into the river. At first, he thought the light that he saw was a reflection of the sun setting on the water, but a split-second later, he realised that the date gardens were on fire. He yelled out.

'Fire! The gardens are on fire!' and he leaped into the air and down the dunes as fast as he could. Behind him, the men turned around in a confused mass and shouts rose into the air alongside the flames. As one, they rushed down the hill, trailed by the elderly imam and those not strong enough to keep up. As they ran through the small streets they heard the screams arise from the houses around them and doors opening on all sides, as the women rushed out carrying buckets, pots and jerry cans of water.

'Stay away from the fire you crazy women!' Babikir Sidahmed yelled as they rushed into the burning forest, the women running alongside them, their tobs dropping off their heads and trailing behind them, drenched by the sloshing water. No one heeded his or anyone else's call, and together the villagers attacked the inferno that was raging in the dry underbrush of the date trees. The animals that were trapped in the flames, tied to the water wheels, were screaming. Overhead, the electricity poles snapped in the heat. Sadig passed a burning hutch of screeching chickens as he dived into the blaze.

The two fires in the village were seen for miles around, their size unprecedented. These villagers were mostly distant cousins, but though they asked one another if they should help, they did not. No. This was an unnatural fire, an unnatural event. We had better stay away and pray for their delivery from whatever evil was in their midst, they told one another.

At the far end of the village, beyond the abandoned ruins, at the foot of the mountain amidst the boulders and crevices, Nyamakeem stood at the open door of her house. She leaned heavily on her staff and closed her eyes as the faint cries travelled up to her, and wondered if this was what she had been waiting for all these years. She stepped back inside her front yard, pushing the door shut. Someone had swept it clean from the leaves that rained down regularly from the Neem tree overseeing the entrance. To her left was a beaten and dried up angereb which she sat in during the day according to the shade and sun. And to the right was the raised platform around her well, in front of the henna bushes.

The boy was bent over the well opening, panting as he drew up the heavy bucket and plonked it over the side.

Wiping his brow, he picked it up and hobbled over to the mazyara. Nyamakeem followed his movements, listening to the sound of the hollow zeer filling up with water. The boy came out again, dropped the bucket back into the well and pulled the cover shut, securing it with a large stone.

'There,' he said, turning to her, smiling shyly. 'I filled the barrel in the kitchen and the one in the backyard as well. There's also a small bucket of water in the out-house.'

Nyamakeem looked at the boy sadly, taking in his wide eyes and short stature. It was like looking at his grandfather thirty-one years ago – except for the chipped tooth. The similarity brought her great pain, and the way it clashed with the boy's sweetness and compassion confused her.

'Aren't you afraid of me?' she whispered. He looked at her blankly, then laughed. A short, sweet laugh from a short, sweet boy.

She knew that he was thinking that she might see the water in his face. What he didn't know was that she saw water in everyone's faces. Here, in this patch of land flanking the river, they were all part of the water, and the water was part of them. They were all a drowning waiting to happen.

And this boy in front of her, with his chipped front tooth and wide forehead, had water painted all over him. He was practically a drowned boy walking.

Nyamakeem sighed and closed her eyes. Her head felt very heavy and her back ached. She needed to lie down. She opened her eyes and looked around her. The front yard was littered with leaves blown into piles all over the place. The water barrels were half empty. The boy was gone.

Eight

It was almost dawn when Hamid Kheir Alseed pushed open the front door and, exhausted and covered in soot, stepped into the front yard of his house. His nephews filed in behind him and trooped towards the bathrooms, the kitchen, and some straight to their rooms or dropped into the beds set up in the verandah. Their mothers and sisters emerged, and the yard briefly bustled with people and talk before everyone headed to their section of the estate, leaving the silence behind them. No women from the Kheir Alseed household had joined the villagers to put out the fire. Hamid pushed the door shut and leaned his forehead against the metal in an attempt to cool his hot skin and burning rage.

He knew what the villagers thought of him and couldn't care less. They were ignorant, superstitious and lazy; all of them. And he knew that for the most part, their contempt was a result of their jealousy of his wealth, of his family's status and his power. They wanted what was his, and he had thought that they would never have it. But now, with everything he had lost, he was almost on the same level with that idiot camel herder and the other pitiable scum of the village. He had lost his own and his family's entire livestock that morning from the mysterious sickness: over one hundred sheep, three dozen high quality goats and a similar number of cows. Their number was so large that they had to be kept in separate pens and areas, and each had their own keeper. And now, all the trees were gone. And before it all: his son.

He had mixed feelings about the boy's disappearance. One of the children who had been with him said he saw the boy run for the fields to hide from punishment, and Hamid thought that was a likely scenario. He would have been doing something foolish by the river and was afraid of what Hamid would do if he found him. And now that the entire village was out looking for him, he would be especially scared of showing his face. His own son had put him in the situation that Hamid despised the most: relying on someone else for help. And that, in addition to the livestock and the burnt trees, fuelled his anger all the more.

He heard a sound behind him and turned around. His mother was standing under the veranda roof in the low light, looking at him questioningly. He knew what she wanted to know but saying it out loud made it more real. He walked with heavy steps across the yard, up the two steps onto the veranda and slumped down heavily into a chair. He pulled off his blackened cap and flung it out into the yard in disgust. His fatigued brain was churning.

'It's all gone.'

She stared at him in disbelief and leaned against the pillar next to her.

'La ilaha ila Allah!'

'Every last mango, orange and date tree, and the cows and horses as well. All burnt to the ground. It's all gone.'

Hajja Allagiya moaned and held her head. Behind her, Sulafa emerged from the side of the house, her arms and feet dripping with water from her ablutions for Fajr prayer.

She stopped a short distance away from her mother-in-law and looked towards her husband. Hamid had not spoken with her since she had returned from her travels the day before. They had not shared the feeling of grief and loss. Neither had comforted or mourned with the other.

She stood silently in place, looking from mother to son and waiting cautiously for an appropriate moment to ask who was standing watch by the river and if the swimmers would be diving again today. All the chaos about the animals and the fire was reaching her through a blurry haze.

Hajja Allagiya was pacing the veranda, slapping her cheeks in distress. First her grandson, then the animals, and now this.

'How could this happen to us? How could this happen? To *us*?' she whimpered, wringing her hands in disbelief. 'What on earth could kill so many animals in one night? What could cause such a hellish fire?'

'I think we both know the answer to that question.'

Hajja Allagiya stopped pacing and turned around to face Hamid. Mother and son glared at each other in the growing light. Behind them, the sounds of clinking glass and rattling cutlery in the kitchen fractured the silence as the women prepared the morning tea and an early breakfast, and heated water in large aluminium pots to pour in steel buckets for the men to bathe from. After a while, Hajja Allagiya spoke in a low voice:

'Half the village has lost their livestock and gardens,' she said, as she sat down heavily on the edge of the bed nearest to her. 'It's not just us who has been affected by this calamity.'

'But none of them are missing their child,' her son answered scathingly. True, but many of them had lost children in the past, his mother thought, though she kept this to herself. Like her daughter-in-law, she was afraid of unleashing her son's wrath. He had never raised his hand against her, but had broken half her furniture in fits of rage.

'What are you talking about?' Sulafa ventured in a small voice. 'Who did this? Has someone done something to Mohamed?'

They both ignored her. Save the clatter coming from the kitchens, the sound of the rest of house's residents had died down almost completely as they settled into sleep after the eventful night. The air was still heavy with smoke, and they could hear the faint sound of weeping from houses down the street.

'She must pay for this.'

'No!' Hajja Allagiya snarled, slapping her hands against her thighs and standing up to her full height. She towered over her son. 'I forbid you. No more bloodshed.'

Hamid did not move, did not unclench his fists. His face was contorted and his left eye was twitching; his breath coming and going in raggedy bouts. He glowered up at his mother but did not say anything more. Sulafa looked in confusion from one face to the other. She couldn't see how all this was more important than her missing son. She had no idea who they were talking about; but then, she had always been an outsider, and no one had ever told her the village stories. Could this person possibly be involved in Mohamed's disappearance? Who could do such a thing? Whatever the answer, Sulafa knew that she wouldn't get it from these people.

Fatima wrung her large scarf from the water, flapped it open and hung it up to dry on the wire clothesline in the alley along with the other clothes she and her parents had been wearing that night. The clothes needed to be washed with soap and rinsed several times to get the soot and smell of burnt animal flesh out of them. She heard her father moving around in his room, and soon heard his footsteps as he stepped out, crossed the yard and headed out the front door. It shut with a clang behind him. Fatima wondered how he could still stand on his legs after being awake since dawn of the preceding day, and particularly with all the running around that had occurred since then. He wasn't young anymore. But there was business to be discussed and it was actually a good thing that he was involved, being one of the few sensible men in their village. With all the drama that had been happening over the last two days tempers were flying and decisions were being made in haste.

It would also keep Mohamed Altahir's mind off their own loss. Fatima's family didn't own any livestock except for the goat and her two kids that they kept at home for milk. They relied completely on the small plot of date trees that was their inheritance from their father's side, and another set of mango trees Mohamed Altahir had bought and grown over the years. The income from the sale of the fruit was good but irregular; the fruits were harvested in September, and there were dry seasons in between where their lunch tray wasn't as full. But Habiba grew different types of vegetables in the yard under the Neem tree, and they always had fresh goat milk and eggs, so it wasn't bad at all. It was a quiet, predictable life.

But Fatima longed for more. The slow pace of the village had always bored her, but now boredom had turned into suffocation. She found it challenging to keep up with the conversation when in the company of the other girls who – not unlike the other Fatima – had nothing better to talk about but what was going on in the village, and whose highest and only aspiration was to get married and have children. At school, she worried Sit Amna with her constant questions which the teacher had no idea how to answer. There was only one school for girls in their village, built by one of the generous capitalists of the area. Until recently it had been only a primary school, and most girls were pulled out by the sixth grade anyway.

Fatima had been to the town of Karima twice with her parents, and both times had come back to her village with the feeling that she had been to the future and was now crawling back into the past. There she had seen more cars on the streets than she had seen in her whole life, the hospital with its high ceiling wards and large flower beds and trees, the bustling market that ran daily and not just twice a week, and the famous Karima railway station with its grand, gleaming train. There were over a dozen schools for boys and girls. And most importantly, there were the young and old women in their sparkling white tobs, carrying their handbags, walking to and from their workplaces at government offices, the bank, the training institutes and the post office. Fatima knew that she wasn't the only girl in her village who aspired to wear that white tob, who wished for something beyond high school. But they all gave up on that aspiration so easily. Even Sawsan, who used to at least entertain Fatima's endless questions and always had her back when she faced the other girls' ridicule, had dropped out the minute her engagement to Omar had been finalised. She wasn't even married yet and was already talking like a boring woman. There were only two other girls in Fatima's class now, and the only reason they were there was because they hadn't been proposed to yet.

The stories Fatima read of the world beyond their village further intensified her unsatiety and made the streets look smaller and the walls closer. The highlight of her month was the day Haj Adam dropped off her new books, but the books were so small and finished in less than two days. She also had the newspapers which she and Habiba took turns reading after her father read them the headlines, which brought them news closer to home: from Khartoum, where the only constant thing was change, so unlike their village which was so static it could have been set in stone.

Fatima was twelve years old when the 1985 April Revolution had toppled the Nimeiri regime, but she remembered every single detail. She had followed the updates daily and questioned her father relentlessly about the events leading up to the revolution: Nimeiri's shifting alliances and Islamist policies, the economic austerity program that made prices shoot up, the war in the South flaring up over a decade after the Addis Ababa agreement had quelled it. Then the associations – doctors, lawyers, university lecturers – calling for demonstrations and strikes, and something they called 'civil disobedience' which Habiba had explained in a whisper was like her and Fatima simply not listening to Mohamed Altahir and forcing him to do his own washing and cooking. Then the army stepping in and taking over while the president was on a trip to America.

All this happening in that big city, by people who weren't that different from her. But it was like they were in a different country. And she knew how she could join them. She knew she almost had the ticket that would take her out of this village and into that city. Despite everything happening – the animals, the fire, the drowning – Fatima could not forget that her final year results were due any day now. She knew that she had a difficult discussion coming up, because she was not going to put those results back in their envelope and into a drawer and forget about them forever. She was not going to become just 'Sadig's wife' forever. She was going to do something with her life, and that something would start when she left this place.

Fatima hung the last bit of clothing then tipped the steel washing basin over, emptying the water near the wall. She picked up the battered tray they used to carry the washing on and leaned it against the wall behind the door leading to the kitchen. She was exhausted. Every bone in her body hurt. The air was heavy with smoke, and with their house being directly adjacent to the gardens the smell was the strongest. Habiba was in the tukul clattering her pots and pans, getting things in order so that they could prepare breakfast and lunch to distribute among the afflicted houses in the neighbourhood. She also appeared to be in some state of denial over the loss of their only source of income. Fatima watched her wiping their largest pot and place it on the biggest coal burner, break up the dry date fronds, push them into the stone stove, cover them in coals and light them with a match. She leaned low and blew until the branches caught fire then pushed them further in. Soon the room was full of smoke.

'Bring out the sack of onions from the storeroom so that we can start preparing this gravy for the meat stew,' Habiba said to Fatima over her shoulder as she stirred the huge tub of wet dough for the gurasa. 'We'll have to tell the baker to send us extra bread as well, and not the burnt ones. On the way back, you need to pass by your aunt Khadija and get the rest of my trays from her –'

She stopped abruptly as she looked up at Fatima, the latter's eyelids drooping as she struggled to keep herself upright. Habiba straightened up and looked at her with pity.

'Why don't you go and lie down for a couple of hours? I can manage this first part on my own.'

Fatima didn't wait to be told twice. She shuffled out of the kitchen into the yard, already half asleep. On the way to her room she stopped abruptly and turned to look at Khalid's closed door. Without much thought, she pushed it open and stepped inside, pushed the door closed behind her and collapsed on his bed. A faint smell of his came to her when she put her head down on the pillow. She didn't think the bedsheets would retain his smell all this time. Perhaps her brain was playing tricks, but she didn't mind; even the illusion of his smell was enough to give her both comfort and sorrow at the same time. She was asleep before her eyes were closed.

She was plunged into the dream at once, as if it had been prowling around in her subconscious, waiting for her. She was standing in the water hut and it was dark and quiet. Everyone else in the house was asleep and she had got up to get a drink of water. She had just pulled the steel cup out of the zeer filled with water and was turning around to go back to her bed; when she heard the front door shut softly behind her and turned around to see Khalid standing in the small doorway, looking in at her.

Fatima felt her heart suddenly fill up, as it always did whenever her dead brother came to her in a dream. She wanted to throw the cup from her hand and jump into his arms and hold on tight. She wanted to chain him to the walls and lock him in the room so that he could never, ever escape again. But she didn't do anything. She just looked at him with mild interest.

It was a young Khalid, around fourteen, several years younger than he was when he had drowned. She felt younger too, somewhere around eight or nine. Khalid was looking at her, but it looked like he didn't know who he was talking to.

'I saw her,' he said. 'The one that Haboba Asha used to tell us about.'

'What?' Fatima asked. Haboba Asha, their maternal grandmother, used to tell them all sorts of stories at night, most of them terrifying and inappropriate for young children and not at all suitable for bedtime. She had passed away almost ten years ago.

'That woman who walks the streets at night. I saw her just now. She was just standing there,' he told her in a shaky voice, 'as if she had been waiting for me.'

Fatima opened her eyes, fully awake despite her exhaustion. The dream felt real, like it was a memory that she had lived and then forgotten. She stared at the ceiling, at the corners with their dusty cobwebs, at the dark stains over the bulging wood where the rainwater had leaked through. Khalid had seen that woman too. He was the one who had told Sawsan about that bastardized prophecy; it had to have been him. But it still wouldn't explain how he could die drowning.

Khalid had drowned in the mild waters of Old Dongola, about a day's distance from their village, where he had been escorting an archaeology expedition. They had been crossing the river and their small boat had capsized, and only two of the nine passengers could swim. Khalid and Daoud, the local guide, had grabbed whoever they could and pulled them up onto the upside-down boat or kept their heads above the water until the men who had been waiting for them on the shore had reached them. Miraculously, everyone survived, except Khalid, one of the best swimmers in the village. Khalid who had been swimming since he was two years old had drowned, and no one could understand it.

Suddenly, Fatima was standing in front of the old woman's front door, looking up at the rusty zinc contraption held to the walls with faded strips of old wood. She had never been there before and had no idea how she knew this was her house. The woman – the soothsayer - was standing next to her, looking at her intently. Fatima tried and failed to close her eyes and cover her ears so she wouldn't hear the whisper. But when she met the old woman's eyes, she was surprised by what she saw. The old woman looked at the young girl, and the young girl looked at the old woman for what seemed like a very long time. Then the old woman and her house vanished as Fatima was shaken awake by her mother.

'Get up, Fatima.'

Fatima emerged in bits and pieces from the second dream and back into the sunshine filtering through her brother's room window. The rusty zinc door dully reflected the sunlight for a second before it changed back into the blue beaten metal rectangle that it was.

'What? What time is it?' she said groggily. She felt like she had slept for just seconds and her head was still heavy with exhaustion.

'Get up Fatima! We have to go!'

She heard the urgency in her mother's voice and sat up to look at her.

'Ummi? What's going on? Has something happened?'

Habiba was crying and pulling her hair.

'It's Sawsan. Oh Fatima, it's Sawsan!'

Nine

Fatima saw her mother's chest rise and fall heavily, saw her slap her face, saw her bewildered look as she stared around the room, before she turned around and hurried away. All sound had disappeared. It was as if the world around her had just turned off, like her father's radio when its battery died. First the air would be full of static and voices from different channels merging into each other, then it would suddenly fall silent.

She swung her legs over the side of the bed and stood up slowly. Her head felt so heavy she thought it would topple her over. She turned towards the door and stepped out into the sunshine. The sky was a perfect and uninterrupted blue. Daylight had come once again, and the night was a thing of the past. She slowly crossed the yard towards the back door on legs of wood, pulled it open and stepped out into the back road. Several women and girls were rushing ahead of her. Some of them called to her and said something, a couple of them embraced her, weeping. She heard nothing and did not respond, but continued walking towards Sawsan's house. She didn't realise that she wasn't dressed in a tob or even a scarf and was walking barefoot.

Down the road, turn right, down the second road, then left. Third house on the right with its back to the small hill on which the abandoned pigeon house stood, and where Fatima had been recently perched, trying to see if Mohamed's body had been found. Had it been just two days ago? Fatima wondered blankly, as she shuffled through the open door and into the yard of Sawsan's house. It felt like it had been a lifetime ago. Several lifetimes, actually.

Standing in the middle of the yard, Fatima calmly observed the scene around her. There were so many people – all women – more than had been present at the Kheir Alseeds' that day. They were moving all over the place, embracing each other and slapping their faces. She could see the exhaustion in their features and could clearly discern the weariness from the sorrow in each face. She stood in place, arms hanging by her sides, as they came to her and hugged her, said things to her, things she couldn't hear. Fatima – the other Fatima – emerged from the crowd and came to her. She was crying hard, her nose running and her mouth hanging open, and Fatima thought that she had never seen her like that before.

Fatima moved through the crowd towards the room that they had been in together just a few hours earlier. The door was open and she stepped inside. The smell hit her immediately: the bride's room smell, heavy with perfume. It took a while for her eyes to adjust to the low light and to understand what it was she was looking at, or looking for. The suitcases they had packed the previous evening were on top of the wardrobe. The incense burner and coal iron were where she had left them on the windowsill, the burnt piece of green silk still stuck in place. The two beds were occupied; several women sat on one, and on the other bed lay a figure wrapped in a floral tob, with four women around it: her mother was one of them, and her aunt Khadija – Sawsan's mother – was the other. On the floor under the bed Fatima could see the glass jars of frankincense and khumra lined up and peeping out under the bedsheet. Khadija looked around and saw Fatima standing by the door and, rocking back and forth and weeping heavily, beckoned to her to come forward. Fatima took two heavy steps towards her and stopped. Khadija stood up and moved towards her with outstretched arms, and Fatima's eyes fell on Sawsan's face.

She didn't look like she was sleeping peacefully. She looked like she was screaming. Her darkened mouth was open and her forehead was creased. Her eyes were half open, the exposed whites crisscrossed with dark red veins. Fatima had seen dead people before, had washed and shrouded them herself. She had never seen someone who had died looking like this.

Suddenly, the world turned itself back on again. A torrent of noise crashed into Fatima from all sides. From far away she could hear screaming, coming closer until it was all she could hear. Only when she felt the women pressing into her from all sides and shaking her did she realise who it was coming from.

❧

Sadig stood at the door to their house, cocking his ear. He could hear wailing nearby. There had been crying since the animals died but this sounded new. Had someone died? Was it old Haj Adam? He sighed and pushed the door shut and walked slowly across the yard to his room. He could hear his mother and sisters on the other side of the house, and another voice – a neighbour or cousin – talking dramatically about something. Utterly exhausted and in no mood to talk to anyone he slipped into his room and quietly shut the door. He was too tired to undress so he kicked his muddy markoub off and turned around to drop down into bed, only to find it occupied. He cursed.

'The cat burnt its tail,' Osman, Sadig's nephew said, holding out Tijani Sidahmed's ugly cat. Sadig hated that animal. It was black and grey with patches of hair missing over its ears making it look like a balding old rat. It was always jumping into people's yards and putting its paws and mouth into any food or milk left exposed. Whenever he looked at it he got the feeling that the cat's yellow eyes were peering deep into his soul, unimpressed with what they saw down there.

'Get that animal out of my face and get off my bed!'

Osman jumped up and moved out of the way as Sadig flopped down onto his back, feeling like a sack of bones barely held together. Outside he heard the clamour of the women leaving through the back door, to the funeral he assumed.

'I found him hiding behind the henna bushes,' Osman continued, stroking the cat's back. 'His tail looks burnt,' he added again.

Sadig covered his face with his arm and breathed deeply, trying to hold his temper. His young nephew was seven years old and stuck to him like a tick to a camel's hide. He followed Sadig around everywhere: to the mosque for prayers, to the gardens for caring for and harvesting the dates and citrus fruits, to the market on Mondays and Thursdays to buy their necessities and haul it back on Sadig's donkey cart. The only place he didn't go – much to his chagrin –

was on the camel rides up north. But he had only a year left, as he reminded Sadig regularly with a grin that was missing several teeth, because when he turned eight years old he would be allowed to join them. And he was going to ride behind Sadig on his camel, of course.

'See this part where there's no hair anymore? And it looks like it hurts because he won't let me touch it.'

Sadig tried to ignore Osman and go to sleep. He strained to block out the images flashing in front of his eyes: the towering flames hungrily eating up the trunks and branches, the canopy of fire over their heads. The smell of smoke and burnt animal flesh. His own skin and feet burning as branches and stalks fell from above.

'If I don't grow up to be like you, I'm going to be a doctor for animals. Then I would be able to find out why the animals died.'

Sadig opened his eyes with a sigh. It was sometimes better to let Osman say whatever it was he wanted to say in order to get rid of him faster. Resigning, he moved a little to the side, and Osman immediately jumped in and snuggled down comfortable next to him, still holding that damned cat. Sadig could always tell him off and kick him out, but he never did, which was why the boy preferred him over his other uncles. The closest he had ever gotten to chastising Osman was when he had been caught playing alone in the abandoned ruins at the edge of the village a year ago. The place was crawling with spiders and scorpions and strange men, and he knew he wasn't allowed there. Sadig had dragged him out by the ear and smacked his behind with a green date frond he had had with him. Osman had run all the way home, crying, but not before he had given

Sadig a look of such hurt and incredulity that it had burnt a hole through Sadig's heart.

Osman chattered on about his plans for the future and his theories about what had killed all the animals. Strangely, none of them involved sorcery, even though Osman had heard of the witch in the mountains just like every other child in their village. Through the haze of exhaustion, Sadig half-listened to Osman's reasoning, and found it surprisingly scientific. Osman thought that whatever had killed the animals was something in the water. Not something that someone had put in the water; something that was already there.

'So why didn't it kill the rest of us?' Sadig snorted.

'We don't drink water from the canal, we get our water from the wells.'

Sadig finally uncovered his eyes and stared at the ceiling. This theory had been the first and strongest among the villagers and was the one that made the most sense. But no one could pinpoint what exactly was wrong with the water in the canal except that there was 'something' in it. That theory also fit comfortably with the second theory of a supernatural force being behind this event of mass death, if not by a direct curse then by cursing or poisoning the water. Yesterday evening as they watched the animals burn, Sadig had listened to the men talking among themselves about the evil sorcery lurking in the darkness. But he had also heard the low discussion about the possible kind of poison that could be in the water: it couldn't be the new insecticides that the agricultural guides had tried to convince them to use, because the villagers had refused to even try them. It was also unlikely to be something that someone had put in the canal because the canal in question was a primary one: it drained directly from the river and its current would be too strong for any poison to retain enough concentration to kill all these animals. There was no logical explanation; it had to be supernatural.

Sadig may not have been as bright as the others. He hadn't completed his education, but then, only a handful of boys in his village had, and none of them pursued any further studies anyway. But he had something that few of the villagers had: experience of the outside world. He and his cousin Abbas were the only men from the village to join the camel convoys, a profession they had been introduced into with the help of Babikir Sidahmed. Babikir sold his camels every two years through intermediaries in the Tangasi market. He had introduced the boys to one of the trail bosses who had taken a liking to them and had agreed to let them join their ranks. From Tangasi, convoys of anywhere between fifty and two hundred camels would travel north for seven to ten days to Egypt, passing by Dongola, Halfa, Deraw and finally ending in Cairo. They would meet other convoys on the way near the border, mainly those coming all the way from Darfur and Kordofan on the ancient Darb Al Arbai'n, or 'Way of the Forty' as that trip took around forty days.

The money Sadig earned from each trip was more than what any other villager earned save the Kheir Alseeds and a handful of others with connections to the influential Khatmiya party. But with the constant devaluation of the Sudanese pound and the economic down-spiralling the Nimeiri regime had caused, prices were constantly rising. This was especially true in their far-flung village, where they relied on neighbouring villages and towns for procurement, and so Sadig had never managed to accumulate much wealth. He was still struggling to finish his matrimonial home which he would move into with Fatima. Still, the trips were well worth it, if not for the income then for the exposure: the different kinds of people he saw, the languages he heard, the strange customs and norms that changed with each village they passed. Learning how to keep the camels within the herd, patch sore camel pads, hobble them at night and avoid potential camel thief hiding spots. The excitement of meeting the camel-riding runners of contraband who appeared out of and disappeared into thin air, smiling slyly, smuggling animal hides, ivory and artefacts stolen from the Pharaonic tombs scatted all over the area. And most importantly, the news that he heard, including whispers about Western countries' poisonous waste material being buried in the desert of the Northern Province with the blessings of the Sudanese presidents, and not just Nimeiri.

Sadig looked over at Osman, still holding that stupid cat and chatting about his grand plans for the future. A future that required a proper education, which Sadig knew was beyond what their village could offer. Whenever he returned from his trips he was always surprised by how small the village was, how static and resistant to change. It was like stepping back in time. But he felt no pressing need to change anything or to go somewhere else. He was comfortable here, except for the worsening poverty, which the whole country was experiencing. And he knew that change would come to them sooner or later, no matter how much they resisted. He could wait.

The cat looked Sadig steadily in the eye, as if following

his thoughts, no intention of going anywhere. Sadig was contemplating throwing it out of the room when he heard banging on the front door and Abbas calling his name.

Sara screamed.

'Move out of the way girl, you're blocking the light.'

The midwife bustled around importantly, arranging her equipment and pieces of cloth, her assistants opening bags and bottles and bossing the onlookers around. Hayat stepped away from in front of her younger sister Om Salama who was holding up the kerosene lamp. Hajja Allagiya sat on a low stool in the corner of the room, her arms crossed and elbows on her knees. She looked like she was hugging herself, and the expression on her face was that of someone who had swallowed something too big and was now finding it difficult to breathe. She watched the chaos of movement in front of her without comment – something that rarely happened, as she always had something to say. The only time she looked up and made any kind of expression was when she saw Sulafa standing at the door, watching the ongoings with the rest of the household women.

'Sulafa!' she barked, making everyone jump and look around. Sulafa started guiltily and, catching the terrifying look on Hajja Allagiya's face, cringed and slinked away in hot embarrassment. She knew she wasn't welcome there but couldn't help coming. She hadn't been allowed to attend either of Sara's deliveries before and there was no reason why this time it would be any different. In fact, this was probably the most important delivery yet. The family worried that Sulafa's bad luck would rub off on Sara and she would fail to get pregnant again. Or that her jealousy of Sara would poison the air around her and cause harm to the mother and the child. She had not been allowed to hold the girls when they had been born and Sara would not breastfeed them while she was present at first. It was as if Sulafa's secondary infertility had given her magical powers of immense wickedness that would dry up Sara's milk and womb.

Sara screamed again, a long, gurgling scream that became hoarse at the end and disintegrated into the air. The contractions were almost continuous and their intensity was at its peak. Sweat and tears streamed down her face, and with each tightening of her abdomen her back arched painfully and she lifted herself off the bed in which Hayat and Hajja Bakhita kept her in and kept her from falling out. The bedsheets underneath her were soaked with blood and amniotic fluid, and with some of the contractions, the smell of faeces mixed with them.

As a mark of the Kheir Alseed's superiority, the delivery was conducted in Sara's room on her large metal bed, as opposed to the traditional method of delivery where the pregnant woman would hold onto a piece of rope hanging from the ceiling and poise over a pit in the ground where the midwife was positioned. Other women in the village and the villages around them still delivered that way. But in the bigger towns and cities, women were now delivering lying down in their homes and even in the hospital. The Kheir Alseeds were no less than these modern city people, and their womenfolk delivered their babies the modern way.

The midwife tapped Sara's thighs and pushed her knees

apart firmly. Usually, this process would be accompanied by pinches and slaps and colourful language, but she wouldn't dare do any such thing with Hamid Kheir Alseed's wife and under Hajja Allagiya's watchful eye.

'Keep your buttocks on the bed and open your legs, I need to see where the head is!'

Sara squeezed her legs shut, writhing and rolling on her back, reaching above her head from the metal headboard to hold onto. Her eyes rolled sightlessly in their sockets and her breathing hitched and caught: every breath made the pain worse. She called out for the hundredth time to Allah to deliver her from this pain or take her soul and end her misery.

'Open your legs! You're squeezing this child to death!'

The midwife motioned to her assistants and the girls grabbed each knee and expertly pried Sara's legs open. She inserted her fingers into the cervix and felt the first baby's head as it crowned. She pulled her hand out and wiped it on the cloth next to her then reached for the razor blade.

'Hold her tight,' she ordered, and all four women around Sara held a limb and pinned it down, turning their faces away from the scene they knew all too well, had experienced themselves and the horror of which they felt with every inch of their being, as the air over their heads split open with Sara's screams fit to raise the dead.

The shrieks were heard all the way across the yard, around the back of the house and into Sulafa's room where she sat on her bed with her back to the door. She cringed involuntarily, knowing full well what the loudest scream of all meant. It was one of the many intolerable burdens of their womanhood that plagued their existence, and one which they continued to inflict on their own daughters despite all the misery it caused them in every stage of their lives. Sulafa knew that the same Sara who was being cut open right now to allow the passage of the babies would be happily distributing sweets and gifts in a couple of years as she celebrated the circumcision of her own girls. She vowed – not for the first time – to never let her own daughter go through such a thing if she was ever blessed with one. A vow that she knew would be useless, because it would never be her decision, but Hajja Allagiya's.

Sulafa hunched down, trying to block out the noise without using her hands that were holding the small garment in her lap. It was Mohamed's naming ceremony gown. It had been made by Hajja Allagiya herself, from pure white cotton embroidered around the neck with white thread. She brought it up to her face and smelled deeply, her tears wetting the delicate cloth. It still smelled faintly of sandalwood. She remembered how she was cleaning out her old clothes a few months ago and had dug the gown out from the bottom of the metal trunk where she kept her valuables and had wondered how tiny Mohamed had been and how big he had grown now. He had been seated at the foot of her bed, bending over his broken sandal which he was trying to fix.

'Do you remember this?'

He looked around at her, and for a second in that frown of concentration she had seen his father, and her heart had leaped into her throat. A second later Hamid had disappeared, and the chipped tooth gaped widely in his laughing mouth as he looked at the tiny gown in her hand.

'Is that mine? I was so small!'

'Yes, you were. You weighed less than a little chick. Your father could hold you in one hand.'

She remembered exactly how he had looked on that day, how he had smelled, how soft his tiny feet had been and how shrill his hungry cries were. There had been a tiny Quraan book sewn into a leather pouch and placed under his blanket to keep him safe. His eyebrows and eyes had been lined with black kohl making him look like a little old lady. She remembered what she had looked like, too: dressed in silk, weighed down with gold bracelets and necklaces and earrings, hands and feet covered in elaborate black henna drawings all the way up to her elbows and knees like a newlywed bride. Both Hamid and Hajja Allagiya had gifted her large sets of gold, and similar gifts were presented to her from relatives and in-laws celebrating the first grandson who would carry the Kheir Alseed name. Her father had also sent her a gift: a modest gold bracelet. Usually, her first child would have been born in her own father's house and she would have stayed with her mother and sisters for forty days after birth. But as she had no mother, and had received no invitation from her father or stepmother to do so, she had shamefully stayed put amidst the whispers and questions of the neighbourhood women.

Mohamed had laughed as he held up the gown and made it dance.

'But why did you make me wear this dress! This looks like the same dress Allagiya and Mahasin wore.'

'Your grandmother made it for you. Everyone was so happy that day. I was so happy.'

She had laughed at his amusement and reached out to take the garment back. But instead, she had put her arms around him and pulled him close to her in a tight hug, felt his short hair rub against her cheek and his wriggling frame trying to get loose. She had held tighter still, ignoring his giggles of embarrassment and his announcements that he was too big for this now. She had held on as tight as she could and wouldn't let him go.

Looking down at her empty arms now and the tiny gown fluttering lightly in the breeze coming in through the open door, she could still feel his small body as if he was there. But she wasn't so sure if she really had hugged him on that afternoon, all that time ago, or if it was just her imagination telling her stories that she so desperately wanted to believe.

❧

Mohamed Altahir was exhausted. He had lost count of how many hours he had been awake. He couldn't remember the last time he had been up for this long, or when there had been this much chaos in such a short time. Their village was a quiet, normal one, and they led quiet, normal lives. They grew their fruits and herded their animals, traded their produce with neighbouring villages, and married their relatives out of convenience more than anything else. Nothing interesting ever happened to them – unless you counted the few unnatural deaths and occasional scandals that gave the village women food for gossip that lasted several years, and which happened everywhere.

So what was going on? A boy drowning or missing in the river was normal. A few animals dying was not unheard of. Three or four feddans of date gardens catching fire was not unprecedented, especially in the dry season, and especially with the abundance of dry, dead underbrush which people neglected to clean up. But a drowning, followed by mass, unexplained death, followed by the burning of three hundred feddans of gardens, all in the space of two days was not at all normal. And now the death of this girl.

Mohamed Altahir tried − and failed − not to think about his burnt trees and what that meant for them. They had long since used up what little savings they had, because even though they had survived the drought of the early 80s and the catastrophic floods of last year, the country was still reeling from decades of strife and austerity caused by the constant mismanagement of those idiot army generals in power. The effects of the capital's decision were felt most acutely in the peripheries, where each percent increase in the price of fuel was a new knot tied into their shrouds. Still, he was probably luckier than others: with all his children dead except one, he had less mouths to feed.

Mohamed Altahir sat a few metres away from Sawsan's father on one of the roped metal chairs from the co-op. They were seated in the shade of the wall, as the young men in front of them dug small holes in the ground into which the metal poles for the funeral tent would be placed. Everyone was moving slowly, automatically, with little discussion. He didn't see Sadig among them which meant that his nephew was with the grave diggers behind the village. Mohamed Altahir liked the boy and was thankful that his only daughter would be in the good hands of a reliable and responsible husband. With Sadig's experience of life beyond the village, he was possibly the most suitable person for Fatima. But he wasn't sure Fatima thought the same. He knew she had other plans for her life, and while he would never admit it in front of his older brother and relatives, he fully believed she would be successful in whatever she chose to pursue: a teacher? A doctor? A politician even? But he worried that she was too far out of touch with the reality of life in their village and the limits that came with it. Or, it could be that she was too far ahead.

The sound of weeping brought Mohamed Altahir back to the here and now. He looked at Sawsan's grieving father briefly then looked away. Whoever had decreed that men shouldn't cry had obviously never lost a child of their own.

Mohamed Altahir had not wept when Khalid had died. At first, it had been out of shock. Like Habiba, he usually took a while to process sudden or bad news. But unlike Habiba he was able to communicate clearly throughout the initial blur and maintain the impression of holding it together. The shock of hearing about Khalid's death had taken longer than usual to subside, during which he had calmly asked about the details of the drowning, the exact location, who had been there, how they had found out. Then he had been mobbed by the masses of men and women who had swept in to weep and pay their respects. It was difficult to cry when you were endlessly shaking hands, slapping shoulders, raising your palms in prayer and responding to the barrage of questions coming from all directions. Soon after that, they had had to travel to where Khalid had drowned to see where he had been buried. They had taken the bus through the desert for a full day, then jostled around in the back of a pickup truck that took them east towards the river where the guides were waiting for them, who crossed them over in the same boat that had tipped its occupants over a few days earlier. Looking down at the grave, he remembered wondering: could they be sure that this was even their son?

'To Allah we belong and to Allah we return,' the men told them as the hysterical Habiba prostrated over the grave and pushed her face down into the dirt, and Fatima knelt down next to her weeping into her hands. They took Mohamed Altahir's silence as a sign of patience, acceptance, or maybe disbelief. But he was in none of those states. He was bothered how the men were sure whose grave it was that they were crying over. The ground was lined with dozens of them, and this one looked just like the others.

Back at home, he had stood in the middle of Khalid's room and looked around. There were three beds: one for each son they had borne, only one of which had shown signs of being slept in regularly. The other two hosted Khalid's many friends and cousins. The legs of the beds were bashed and scraped from the hundreds of trips out to the yard and back inside, depending on the weather. Mohamed Altahir had stared down at Khalid's bed for a long time, his eyes obstinately dry, not a single tear daring to escape. And he had thought to himself: so, this is what it feels like to lose a child – to have a child taken away from you.

He had stepped out of the room, pulled the door shut behind him, and never set foot in it again.

'Such a strange way to die,' Haj Mutasim said. Mohamed Altahir assumed his older brother was addressing him, though it sounded as if he was wondering aloud to himself. He straightened up in his chair and drummed his fingers nervously on his knees, sensing trouble.

'They should never have given the girl the Western medicine. That's what was behind it all. What do those fools in Khartoum know about these things?'

'They had already tried everything else,' Mohamed

Altahir said in a low voice, looking sideways at Sawsan's father and motioning to his brother to lower his voice. 'This is hardly the time to discuss these matters ya Haj.'

Haj Mutasim took no notice.

'These strange illnesses that are touches of the djinn, they need to be healed with Quran and zikr, not with bottled chemicals and concoctions brought to us by the infidels. We've known this for centuries and have been taking care of our people with the tools we know best. It's the way we've always done things. It's the way we should always do things.'

The men around him were quiet, looking from Haj Mutasim to Sawsan's father, who was sitting upright in his chair and glaring at the old man with glistening eyes.

'The Western medicine was the only thing that controlled her illness. Before it she couldn't go a single week without having a seizure. She was doing so well, we all forgot what it was like before. After all these years she was finally leading a normal life.'

He leaned back heavily and looked away, his chest heaving.

'Six years ago, we would never have imagined that she could get married. We thought that she would be trapped in her illness forever.'

Haj Mutasim was relentless.

'So what happened then? Why did they suddenly come back?'

'Ya Haj,' Mohamed Altahir said, putting his hand on his brother's arm and looking at Sawsan's devastated father in embarrassment. In a lower voice, he said 'the man is mourning his daughter's death, this is no time for unsolicited advice. Besides, what good is any of this talk doing? The girl is with her Maker now.'

Haj Mutasim leaned forward on the stick between his knees and opened his mouth, then sat back in his chair in silence. Mohamed Altahir sighed in relief. Then:

'This just shows us that when we part from our ways we fall into calamity and nothing good comes out of it.'

Mohamed Altahir looked around at Sawsan's father in alarm, but movement at the front door caught their attention. Sadig and several other men, weary and covered in dust, were motioning to them. Mohamed Altahir got up.

'The grave is ready. It's time to bury the girl.'

Ten

A year after Mohamed was born it became evident that another child was expected from Sulafa. And indeed, a sudden attack of nausea and heightened sense of smell announced the impending arrival of another child. As she waved away the bowls of boiled lemon and water brought to her and leaned over the bucket beside her bed to vomit, she wondered: could the love she felt for her Mohamed expand to include the newcomer? Would she have enough space in her heart for the two of them? She had her doubts, but she looked forward to that moment with relish and enjoyed every cringing moment of her morning sickness. Until it stopped.

The first miscarriage was painless, swift, and over in two days. There was nothing to bury; the pregnancy had been too early. She was shocked; too shocked to register the reactions of her husband and in-laws. It had only been seven weeks, but she wept bitterly as the midwife cleaned up around her and packed her things, signalling the end of the affair and hurrying along to her next appointment. Just a month and a half, but she had felt as if she had lost someone she had known all her life. Her child. And while she knew that these things happened, she was surprised that, instead of the sympathy she expected from the household, she found annoyance. And the annoyance turned to outright anger with her second miscarriage. They watched with disgust as she writhed in pain from the cramps and left her alone to clean up the sheets bloodied with bits of flesh and clots.

Then Hajja Allagiya summoned the two village midwives who brought their bags and brews and made her lie down as they ran their humiliating diagnostics.

'Her uterus is too weak.'

'Her blood is too thin.'

'She spends too much time carrying the boy and that has affected her back. No more carrying the boy.'

'There is a blackness around her: an evil eye following her around, polluting her aura and actively working to prevent another successful pregnancy. It would be good to investigate and purge such evil.'

She was brought things to drink: water with verses from the Quran read over it, tonics infused with herbal and animal-sourced blood strengtheners. Her periods were followed closely: were they too long? Too short? Too heavy? Too light? It appeared the medicines were working because there were no following miscarriages. But that was because there were no pregnancies either. For two more years, the days of each month were counted down, the medicines and prayers and incense burning were scheduled and followed, and other people did the work in the house. But no foetus announced its impending arrival, and that was when the beating began.

She remembered the first time Hamid had hit her because it was the day she had received the news of her stepmother passing away. It was also the day Mohamed had fallen off the pigeon house and chipped his tooth. As she soothed the crying boy and stuck her finger in his mouth to retrieve any remaining fragments, she tried to summon tears of her own to mourn Asha Sidahmed Elnour, the woman who had entered and altered their lives so dramatically and yet so subtly that it was as if she had planned it all along. In fact, after all these years and after her own experience in life as a married woman, Sulafa was now quite sure that her stepmother (may her soul rest in peace) had planned it all quite carefully: she had ensnared the newly widowed – and newly rich after inheriting much of his deceased wife's wealth – father before anyone else got to him, swiftly secured the marriage proposal by mobilising the village's informal matchmakers, moved in to an already established house that required little work, and immediately got down to the business of starting her own family. With the abundance of helpful relatives, she hadn't needed to spare much energy on the orphans – the 'other' children – and only needed to show them enough tolerance to maintain the image of a 'good stepmother'. This show was put on mainly for the deceased mother's family since no one else really cared. When it came to marriage, the choices made rarely put the children first, or second or even third. Rarely did a man marry someone for the sake of his children and at the expense of his own personal desires, and this choice would almost always be supported by those around him. So, Asha Sidahmed Elnour was successful in her quest, and even more successful in the eventual dispersion of the children she had inherited from the deceased woman. Her endeavours were met with widespread approval since, especially for girls, what is more honourable than marriage?

So the tears had not come when Sulafa heard the footsteps behind her and the light coming through the door was blocked by the man in the doorway.

'Stop crying this instant, boy.'

Mohamed's cries had come down to a whimper by then, but he suddenly cried even harder, out of fear more than pain, because even at the age of four he had already been at the receiving end of his father's strong hand more than once. Sulafa took him in her arms and turned to face Hamid.

'Leave him. He fell from all the way up there and is lucky to have just chip–'

The blow knocked both her and her son to the ground. She stared at the ceiling, stunned and breathless for a few seconds, then felt the boy being wrenched out of her arms, screaming loudly, before the resounding slap shut him up. Then Hamid grabbed her by the hair and yanked her up and close to his fuming face.

'Don't you dare tell me how to treat my son, woman,' he snarled, his hot breath smelling of okra stew and onions. 'You're the reason he's turning into such a sissy in the first place. Next time you interfere with how I raise my son I'll break your face!'

He threw her back on the ground and stalked out of the room, dragging the screaming boy behind him.

That first time, Sulafa had lain on the ground staring at the ceiling in mild shock. She was shocked he had hit her. But then, she wasn't so shocked. At some level she had always known that something like this would happen sooner or later. She had seen what kind of man he was when he was angry: kicking furniture and animals out of his way, throwing glassware at the wall. If she was someone else she would have sent word home to her father and brothers; she was, after all, the daughter of the Sufi sheikh. But she

118

didn't, because she knew no one would care. Hamid hit her
again when he found an obstinate spot on his jallabiya that
her scrubbing had dimmed but not removed. And again,
when Mohamed refused to jump into the river with the
other children for fear of the slimy eels at the bottom. And
again, when his cousin – who had married one year after
him – announced the birth of his fourth son.

'I don't know what you're waiting for with this one,'
Hajja Allagiya had said one morning as she lay on her side
under the zinc roof of the veranda, sipping her afternoon
coffee with Hamid as Sulafa sat on the far end mending a
ripped pocket. She kept missing the stitch and pulling the
needle back out again as she worked hard to keep the tears
in her eyes from spilling over. She hated crying in front
of them: it drew a smirk from her mother and sisters-in-
law and stoked the ever-burning embers of Hamid's wrath.
They often talked about her as if she was invisible now, and
even made a point of ignoring her presence and talking over
her when she was around.

'She needs to fix her mistakes,' Hamid said with disgust.
'After all that dowry money I paid I should at least be getting
my money's worth.'

'I'm not going to wait forever for another grandson. If
you had listened to me the first time we wouldn't be in this
situation, but it's the fate of this boy who his mother would
be no matter how unfortunate that is.' She threw Sulafa a
dirty look.

The engagement was announced two weeks later, and
Sulafa was moved from her large bedroom and home to a
smaller bedroom at the back of the house. The new bride
was ushered in on the same day her son had been born, five

years earlier. Before the year was over they had a daughter, who was dutifully named after her grandmother, and less than two years after that another daughter. The girls were beautiful creatures, with laughter that sounded like raindrops dripping onto a tea tray laden with English biscuits and expensive china and strong morning tea. Sometimes, when Sulafa was going through a dark phase and was withdrawing into herself, the sound of raindrops would draw her out of her sordid mood and back into the sunshine. They both looked like miniature versions of their mother, with her large eyes and wide forehead. Despite there being several other granddaughters in the house, Hamid's daughters were spoiled by everyone, never admonished for anything, and even their roasted watermelon seeds were peeled and put in a small bowl ready for them to eat.

Even Sulafa couldn't help but feel some affection towards them, though with time she learned to hide this. She would sit in the corner of the room and watch as Khatmallah – whose job was to take care of the neighbourhood women's hair – unbraided the girls' thick pigtails, poured karkar and peanut oil into the hair and massaged it in, combed out the tangles, oiled the hair again then plaited it in long, shiny braids that reached down to their waists. When Sara was sick with her third pregnancy Sulafa offered to wash the girls' clothes for her, not out of any concern for Sara's health but because she wanted to touch the flowery fabric and straighten the dresses that she imagined could be her own daughter's one day. She had still not given up hope of having another child. But this affection was not welcomed either by the mother or the grandmother, and they made it clear that Sara and Hamid's daughters were off limits.

Mohamed on the other hand was shown no such restrictions. On the contrary: the girls adored him and he adored them, and filled the role of the big brother admirably, praised and encouraged by his grandmother in particular. In fact, Mohamed was the only person in that household who was held at a higher status than the girls – higher even than his older cousins. The girls followed him around the house, tried on his sandals when he lay in bed, and climbed onto his back at every opportunity. He pitted their dates for them and chose the best ones, making sure there were no pests hiding inside, and brought the donkeys to the door of their room and took them on rides around the front yard. Whenever Mohamed was around the sound of raindrops on the tea tray filled the house and elevated everyone's mood – even Sulafa's. Mohamed was a main part of the Kheir Alseed family, and his relationship with his sisters – and grandmother, and aunts and cousins – was protected and natural. He belonged with them, in that house, in that family. With the arrival of his sisters, instead of being replaced he was elevated and his position was ensured. The exact opposite of what had happened to his mother.

Sulafa was eventually shut out of the Kheir Alseed family, pushed to the periphery of the household, kept in the corner of the family tree out of necessity more than anything else, being the mother of the only person who would carry the family name – until Sara would give birth to a son. As painful as it was, she didn't find it difficult to accustom herself to this arrangement. After all, it wasn't that different to her life growing up: living a life of unloved existence, a body taking up space but invisible, not introduced to the guests, not missed at the lunch tray. And if there was one good thing that had come out of Hamid's second marriage, it was that he was now too occupied to focus his wrath on Sulafa, and the beating finally ceased.

Eleven

The screaming had stopped. Sulafa looked up and turned her ear to the door, listening for the sound of the babies' cries. There were none. Had she missed it while she was lost in her thoughts and now the babies were happily nursing? It must be so; she felt like she had been dreaming for hours. She stood up and walked towards the door, cocking her ear to listen. She could hear voices but couldn't make out the words. Had Sara given birth to girls? Was that why the air was so subdued? She stepped out cautiously into the yard and walked along the wall towards the corner of the house, looking around her furtively. The voices were louder now: she could hear the midwife, and Hajja Bakhita. Their voices sounded urgent. Sulafa looked around the corner towards the room that was on the other end of the house, the voices louder now. Suddenly a young woman jumped out of the room and without looking in either direction, took off across the yard, pulling her tob on hastily as she ran out the door. Sulafa looked after her in alarm and started as she heard the unmistakable sound of a hard slap.

'Sara! Wake up! Wake up and push God damn you!'

There was no mistaking the urgency now. Sulafa hurried towards the room and looked inside. She was almost knocked over by the smell and sight of blood – there was so much of it, everywhere, over everything. The midwife was standing up, her stool knocked to the ground as she struggled and pulled. One of her assistants was trying to hold up both of Sara's limp legs and when she saw Sulafa at the door she called out to her to help. Without hesitation, Sulafa rushed to the other side and grabbed Sara's other leg, still holding Mohamed's gown which she stuffed hastily into her dress. Sara was lying on her back, not moving but breathing shallow breaths, her arms splayed out limply over the sides of the bed. Her weeping mother was shaking her and alternately tapping and kissing her face, trying to wake her up. Hayat and Om Salama were plastered against the wall, immobile with fear, staring at the Sara's bulging abdomen which had not released its contents yet. The first baby's head appeared to be stuck in the canal.

The midwife slapped Sara's thighs viciously, desperately, pushing on her abdomen and buttocks and manoeuvring her fingers around the small head, trying to pry it free.

'Wake her up and make her push! This baby is suffocating!'

Sulafa looked down at the little purple face that was slowly rotating, dark blue lips open in a voiceless cry. It appeared to have stemmed the gush of blood that had soaked the bedsheets, the floor and the midwife's clothes and hands. She looked back at Sara's placid form and her stomach churned with worry. She heard movement behind her and Hajja Allagiya appeared by her side. She pushed Sulafa roughly out of the way and descended on the unconscious young woman, raised her hand and brought it down on her face so hard she almost knocked her over the side of the bed.

'Wake up!' she screeched, bringing her hand up again.

'You're not killing my grandsons you worthless bitch! Wake up now!'

The resounding slap echoed off the walls.

'Hajja Allagiya!' Sara's mother wailed beseechingly, trying to grab her hand as it rose into the air again. 'Stop! Stop you're killing her!'

Hajja Allagiya wrestled her arm away from the woman and shook Sara roughly with her free hand. Sulafa ducked her head just in time to avoid getting slapped upside the head. She could hear the midwife praying and cursing beside her.

'Give me that razor!' she barked at her assistant. 'I'm cutting this baby out and I don't care if this stupid girl shits out of her vagina for the rest of her life!'

Sulafa watched in horror as the razor swept down and to the side, at which Sara suddenly came to life and let out a blood curdling scream. The wrinkled body was ejected out in a huge gush of bright red blood. The midwife grabbed the floppy body and turned it onto its stomach, slapped its back and buttocks, stuck her fingers into its mouth and swiped out black fluid. She turned it onto its back and placed it into the awaiting bit of cloth the assistant was holding with shaking hands. She massaged the tiny chest and pumped the legs up and down. The women watched fearfully. Sara had collapsed again and was forgotten for the moment. The other assistant who had been dispatched earlier appeared in the doorway, bedraggled and out of breath.

'I sent word to the medical assistant in Karima, but it will take him hours to get here.'

'Never mind him! Cut the cord.'

They tied two bits of string around the umbilical cord

and cut between them, and the immobile baby was wrapped in the cloth for the assistant to revive as the midwife turned back to deliver the second one. Hajja Allagiya called out:

'Is it a boy?'

The midwife ignored her. If she had been in her right mind, she would have masked the look of disgust on her face.

'You! Rub the girl's abdomen and push down!'

Sulafa looked behind her to see who this order was directed at and realised it was her. Quickly, she leaned Sara's leg against her chest and reached over to massage her abdomen, which had visibly decreased in size but was still contorted and lopsided. She felt a small, hard mass under her hand and, bracing herself against the bed, pushed down on it. With horror she saw more blood pour out from between Sara's legs.

'Push again!'

Sulafa looked in panic towards Hajja Bakhita who was holding Sara's head in her arms and weeping. Hajja Allagiya stood motionless, staring steadfastly at the first child who was still being revived by the assistant across the room. Behind her, Hayat was plastered against the wall, and Om Salama had disappeared.

'Push! Push down! The second baby is here!'

Sulafa brought both her hands down and pushed as hard as she could. She felt the hard mass move slightly at first as it faced the resistance of the canal. She felt the lax skin under her hands and waited for two breaths, then felt it harden. She pushed down again.

'Okay stop! Stop pushing!'

The midwife moved her fingers around the baby's neck

and reached deeper inside, pulling out the cord that was twisted around it. She wriggled her fingers underneath it, pulled this way and that then brought it over the small face and head. Sulafa watched the head rotate slowly until it was facing upwards.

'Now push as hard as you can!', the midwife shrieked.

Sulafa put one knee on the bed, hoisted herself up and pushed down with all her weight. She felt the hard mass suddenly give away as the baby popped out and almost lost her balance. This time, they heard the shrill cries loud and clear as the midwife slapped the baby's bottom and cleared its throat. She placed it into the second piece of cloth that was spread out in waiting and rubbed it down vigorously.

'Well?' Hajja Allagiya called out impatiently. 'Are they boys or girls?'

'They're both barely alive if that's what you want to know,' the midwife shot back irritably. She was visibly shaking as she cut the cord of the second child, then turned her attention back to the bleeding mess behind her. The first child had still not cried. Sulafa caught a glimpse of a tiny dark blue foot protruding from the blanket. The huge, knobbly placenta slid out easily, bringing even more blood with it. Sulafa wondered just how much blood one person could have and lose. She looked at Sara's face and cringed: it was completely colourless. The midwife pushed bits of cloth against the flow and one of the assistants handed her a large, curved needle with thick black thread. She started stitching but kept stopping as the blood obscured her view.

'Well?' Hajja Allagiya screeched at her, moving to the foot of the bed and pushing Sulafa out of the way. Behind her, Hajja Bakhita was still cradling Sara's shrinking face.

She hadn't even looked at the babies, nor did she appear to see or hear any of what was going on in the room.

'Sara, Sara, wake up ya bitti!' she cried. Sulafa stood against the wall looking at the mother and daughter, and noticed for the first time just how very young Sara was. She had always known her age, but the small, limp, desecrated form lying exposed in front of her looked like nothing more than a child. Beneath the makeup and henna, she was like a doll that had been dressed in grown-up clothes. A child that had been desperate to give her in-laws – her owners – the children they demanded. Even if it cost her her life. Sulafa stared at the dying girl with pity and felt that they had been more alike than either of them had known.

Sulafa looked down at the midwife who had given up on stitching and was pushing soaked bits of cloth and cotton to try and stem the bleeding, to no avail. Behind her, Hajja Allagiya was peering between the babies' legs. She turned around, took a deep breath and let out a lusty, full throated ululation that rang against the walls. She took no notice of Sara and instead looked straight at Sulafa with a grotesque look of triumph.

'Boys!'

⚯

Sadig coughed as he heaved dirt into the grave. Several other young men shovelled alongside him and the white, shrouded form lying on its side below them disappeared fairly quickly as the hole filled up; as if it was in a hurry to get going, to move on from this world and onto the next. The older men standing around them dispatched their usual torrent of advice about the correct way to bury a body, but Sadig ignored them. He had buried many bodies in his lifetime, both inland and by the water, and felt that his experience in the matters of death far surpassed what was appropriate for his age.

The deceased girl's father was embraced and consoled by the villagers – the same group who had been consoling each other in front of the fire last night. It was as if their grief was being passed around from person to person and they took turns carrying it. Sadig couldn't remember when there had been so much going on in their village. He stepped away from the crowd and walked through the graveyard that was on the outskirts of the village towards the houses. The roads were almost completely abandoned; all the men at the graveyard, all the women at the house of mourning or walking to and from it on the back roads. He walked briskly through the streets, crossed the main road and entered the gardens. Between cleaning up after their night in the gardens and digging and filling the grave for Sawsan, Sadig had been asking questions.

'Where did it start?'

'I don't know where it started,' Mousa had replied irritably. 'I was just sitting there minding my own business and suddenly all hell broke loose around me. It was as if Jahannam's gates had opened!'

Abbashar minded the gardens for most of the villagers and had a small hut on one of the Kheir Alseed plots. He was old and thin but fit from a lifetime of hard work. And most importantly, he had a sharp eye. He had been dramatically reenacting the story of the fire and his heroic role in it for most of the morning, but exhaustion, the magnitude of loss and Sawsan's sudden and ghastly death had stifled his enthusiasm.

'Just think,' Sadig pressed him. He wasn't sure why it was important for him to know exactly where the fire had started. Something was evading him; a thought, an explanation.

'I said I don't know! It started from the water side and moved inwards. That's all I remember.'

Sadig trudged through the hollowed-out gardens, heading towards the water side to the camping site where they had been keeping watch the night Mohamed Kheir Alseed had drowned. The light shone strangely down on him from above; usually, the gardens were shaded and cool, the canopy of palm fronds filtering out the light. But with all the leaves gone, the gardens were naked and exposed. He saw the river from far away because the tall rushes that usually blocked the view had been burnt away as well. The river itself should have evaporated from the heat of last night's fire, but miraculously it flowed on, oblivious to all the lives that had ended on its shores. He emerged from the trees and walked over the flattened land towards the bank. Bits of warped metal marked the area where they had stationed their beds that evening. He bent over and looked closely at the ground, moving the debris around, searching.

He didn't find anything. He was looking for the kerosene lamp they had had with them that night. It wasn't there. He tried to remember where he had last seen it. It had stayed on all night and towards dawn had started to falter as the kerosene ran out, about an hour after Babikir Sidahmed had left. When he had woken Gasim up for his shift, he had moved it to the head of the bed before lying down so that he wouldn't knock it over with his feet when he got up later. Then what? Sadig stared at the ground, racking his brain. They had gotten up together to pray Fajr, and not long after Babikir's nephews had brought down the tray with morning tea, and with it the news of the dead animals, at which they had gulped down their tea and rushed off – and they must have taken the kerosene lamp with them.

Sadig straightened up. The fire wasn't their fault. No one had suggested it, but the possibility had been festering in the back of his mind all day. He stretched his aching back and rubbed his tired eyes. Then his sight fell on an opening in the trees in front of him. That was where Babikir Sidahmed had emerged that night, smelling freshly of cigarettes. Sadig stared at the scorched earth and trees, trying to add up the events in his head, but his brain was lurching along sluggishly, overwhelmed with exhaustion. He turned around and walked towards the river, taking deep breaths. He felt as if the burnt smell that had been following him around since the evening before was stuck to his skin and would stay with him forever. He breathed in the clear air coming in from the river and looked down to his feet to make sure he didn't step onto any crumbling overhang.

And there below him, bobbing up and down with the current, the waves lapping playfully at his face and sides, was Mohamed's puffed-up body.

Twelve

The old Land Rover trundled down the main road of the village, its driver staring out the window at the decimated date gardens that had been verdant and fertile the last time he was here. He slowed to a stop and poked his head outside, looking for someone to ask just what in Allah's name had happened. There was no one to ask, though, which was just as strange. He was always having to slow down to let donkey carts cross or to avoid children kicking their ball and chasing it under his wheels. He started slowly along the road, keeping an eye and an ear out.

Suddenly someone leaped out of the trees in front of his car and he slammed down on the breaks, and the car screeched to a slippery halt on the dirt road. He cursed loudly as the young man sprinted across the road and disappeared into the narrow streets on the other side.

'Look where you're going you animal!'

The aging car spurted and churned but would not start. Cursing again, the driver leaned over and got the crank from behind him. He opened the door and got out, popped the trunk and pushed the crank into the opening, turning it several times until the Land Rover came back to life.

Just as he was straightening up, he heard footsteps behind him, and turned around just in time to avoid being knocked over by the man running in the opposite direction.

'Hey! Watch where you're going!'

Hamid Kheir Alseed took no notice of him, and the man stared after the rapidly receding figure as he disappeared into the burnt trees in a cloud of ash. The man cursed again but could not move out of the way fast enough and was bowled over by the stampede of men and boys rushing across the road and into the gardens, talking excitedly. Someone pulled him roughly up and he flattened himself against the hood of the car.

'What the hell is wrong with you people!'

The crowd thinned but continued, the stragglers older and more dignified, all hurrying in the direction from which the first man had come. A few men shouted out a hurried greeting and slapped him on the shoulder. The driver stared after them. Then he heard a sound from the trees coming from the direction of the river. It sounded like a wounded animal. He cupped his hand to his ear, tapping on his hearing aid.

It wasn't the sound of an animal. It was a man, wailing loudly.

The driver parked the car in front of the school gates. He got out, opened the back door and hauled out a heavy sack which he threw over his shoulder and pushed the door shut. He trudged into the school yard towards the offices. There was no one there, even though it was the middle of the day. He knocked loudly on the unlocked office door, pushed it open, and put his load down onto the desk. He stepped out and looked left and right for any sign of a teacher or administrator. There was no one. Well, it was the summer holidays, so they wouldn't be keeping official office hours. But they should know that this week was the week the Ministry of Education sent out the final results and the mail could arrive any day. Like today, for example.

The driver looked back at the sack on the desk which had opened slightly and ejected a couple of envelopes. He reached down and picked them up, looking at the names: Ahmed Al Haj, Om Alhassan Wad Alsafi, and a Mohamed someone or another. He put the envelope back in the sack and closed it securely. Then he stepped back out again, pulled the door shut behind him, trudged back to his old Land Rover and drove off.

⌒

The house was packed again just as it had been on the day Mohamed had gone missing. But this time the women came and went in waves, alternating between the two houses of mourning. Sulafa sat in shocked stupor on the veranda, in the same seat she had occupied two days before. Her face was colourless, her wide eyes staring at nothing, her clothes splattered with blood, barely covered by the light tob that she had been dressed in by Om Salama. This time, Sara was nowhere to be seen. Hajja Allagiya was in her same position as well, but she maintained none of the haughty dignity of before: she was inconsolable, crying loudly and rocking back and forth; an unusual image that was far removed from her usual cold and disdainful self. She wept and called to her dead grandson as 'Yaba', my father; an expression of endearment, but also of habit: Mohamed had been named after Hajja Allagiya's father. Though Mohamed had been presumed dead for days, it appeared that she hadn't believed it until she saw the body.

Fatima was also in the same position she had been on the morning when Mohamed first went missing. She stood against the pillar and watched the Kheir Alseed household occupants and visitors with disinterest. She felt a detached sense of déjà vu as she looked at the scene playing out in front of her. It was like a replay of one she had seen before, but all the actors had forgotten their lines and roles. She tried not to think about the last time she was here, when Sawsan had sought her out and settled in comfortably next to her. She remembered their discussion on the way home: Sawsan's worry and her annoyance. Tears filled Fatima's eyes as she remembered her ridicule and harsh responses. Couldn't she have been a little kinder?

Sawsan had died.

As the fire had raged in the gardens that evening, the breeze had blown burning leaves and branches towards the nearest line of houses, and with their roofs of dry branches a few of them caught fire. There weren't that many; flooding in 1988 had demolished the houses closest to the river and gardens, but Sawsan's father had quickly rebuilt and moved the family back in, so the house was fully exposed to the flames. Sawsan had stayed at home and had apparently tried to put out a fire on the rakoba, a wooden structure attached to the men's quarters that was made of and covered with dried branches to provide shade. Her mother had come home to refill the water buckets. Khadija had found a trail of splashed water leading to the men's quarters, where she found her daughter lying face-first in a puddle of muddy water and ash, an overturned bucket lying next to her. Her feet were still twitching slightly from the seizure. The rakoba next to her had burnt to the ground.

She had drowned in four inches of water.

Fatima had dragged herself away from Sawsan's house, extracting herself from the suffocating embraces of the women who held her head and shoulders and wailed into her ear. When the time had come to wash and shroud the body, Fatima was unable to lift her arms to pour the water or undo Sawsan's hair and was gently moved aside. She couldn't look into Sawsan's face – it looked nothing like the sweet, laughing Sawsan she had known her entire life. Sawsan was the sister she had never had. She cried as that face disappeared under the white cloth forever, the knots were tied at the head and feet and perfume was sprayed over the shrouded body. The men brought in the low roped bed on which Sawsan would be carried to her final resting place and the body was placed onto it. She was covered with a white tob amidst the rising cries and laments.

Choking and heaving, Fatima had pushed herself away from where she had been wedged in the corner of the room near the window with the iron and incense burner. She had avoided Sawsan's mother's flailing arms as her aunt screamed and slapped her face until she had to be restrained by the other women. She had turned away from the embraces of the cousins and aunts and neighbours reaching out to her, a sea of arms and fingers pulling at her clothes. She had stood over the covered form, trapped in its shroud, unable to escape if it wanted to, unable to return to life if it tried. She had sunk down to the ground near the body's – Sawsan's – feet, put her head onto the bed and cried as the men stood around it, waiting to pick it up and bear it on their shoulders out of the house. She took no notice of Sadig who stood in the doorway and looked down at her bent, uncovered head.

Fatima surfaced from the depth of her thoughts to a silence that had descended on the house like a heavy blanket. It started at the far end of the yard near the front door and sailed over it to the veranda, to the rooms and kitchen inside. She looked around her as the women collectively fixed their gaze on the front of the house. There was a woman standing at the gates.

It was Nasima. But no, Fatima thought as she looked at her. It wasn't Nasima, but whoever she was she was obviously not from the North; she was so tall and dark. Fatima had never seen her before, which was odd, because everyone knew everyone in their village. The woman's tob was hanging low over her face, shading her eyes. Was she someone who knew the family and had come to visit?

The woman stepped into the yard and slowly walked through the crowd. The women moved away and a narrow path was forged between them. She did not look to either side and walked purposefully towards the veranda as if she knew exactly where to go and exactly who it was that she was looking for. Low whispering crackled across the yard like an electric current as she passed, all eyes following her progress with fascination.

Hajja Allagiya, the late Hassan Kheir Alseed's wife, mother to Hamid Kheir Alseed and his three sisters, mother-in-law to Sulafa and Sara, and the richest and most powerful woman in their village, had stood up. In the quiet afternoon air her breathing sounded laboured and she looked angry. No, Fatima thought with alarm: she looked absolutely livid.

'What are you doing here?' she demanded in a hoarse whisper, as she glared at the visitor standing at the foot of the veranda. Her voice was low and thick but carried clearly across the now silent house. The woman said nothing. She stood in silence a few feet away, her eyes still hidden.

'How dare you step foot in this house!' Hajja Allagiya spat furiously. 'What do you want?'

The woman looked up, but not at Hajja Allagiya. Instead, she looked past her to stare at Sulafa, who was sitting up in her chair, gripping its sides and looking alert for the first time. Even with her eyes now visible, the look on the woman's face was hard to decipher, especially with the bright light behind her and the relative gloom of the shaded veranda in front of her. From her vantage point, Fatima saw how the light filtered through the thin material of her tob and fell on her face, giving an impression of freckles. No, they weren't freckles, they were tribal markings over her forehead. The woman was not young, but she couldn't tell how old she was exactly – certainly older than her own parents. On closer inspection she found her less intimidating than she thought before. She studied her face with some urgency. The woman looked surprised. Sad, perhaps.

Sulafa broke the spell.

'Who are you?' she whispered. 'Are you … her? The one they've been talking about? Did you do something to my son?'

'Don't talk to her!' Hajja Allagiya thundered. She took a step forward and pulled herself up to her full height, towering menacingly over the thin woman at her feet, who continued to ignore her and stared into Sulafa's distraught face. Her mouth opened as if to speak, then shut again without a word. Then, sighing audibly, she slowly raised both cupped hands and looked down.

Al Fatiha. A prayer read when paying respects to the relative of a deceased person.

Hajja Allagiya, tears of grief and fury streaming down the crevices in her cheeks, screamed:

'No! Don't you raise your hands to Allah in this house you devil! You witch! Ya wash alshoum! Keep your damned curses and prophecies to yourself! Out! Out of this house now, out!'

The woman seemed not to hear. She continued to stare down at her hands, mumbling under her breath, her own tears starting to seep slowly down her face. Then she slowly lowered them and turned to look up steadily into the black fire in Hajja Allagiya's eyes. The difference in size was remarkable: Hajja Allagiya was obese and wrapped in a stiff tob that amplified her girth. The strange woman – though very tall – was very thin and a little bent. She was draped in an old, dirty, thin tob which might have been white once upon a time, and which was flung over her right shoulder and not her left. Her dusty feet were wrapped in thin plastic sandals, one of them torn and sewn together several times. She wore no gold. Hajja Allagiya advanced on the woman intimidatingly, screeching insults and threats, threatening to throw her out onto the street if she didn't leave. The woman seemed unafraid and met her threats with a cold stare, but turned slowly on her heel anyway. She took one step away, then stopped and turned slowly back around to face the bristling matriarch. She opened her mouth and said something that Fatima couldn't hear over the wailing women in the background, but whatever it was first shocked, then sent Hajja Allagiya into a flying rage. Screeching insults and curses, she bent down to the ground, picked up a fistful of sand and flung it into the woman's face.

The woman closed her eyes to the dust but did not otherwise flinch, and when she opened her eyes again Fatima saw that whatever emotion had been there before was replaced by nothing at all. She looked vacantly at the family, deaf to the tumult around her, then turned around and walked back down the yard, her frame shrinking in the swamping sea of screams and cries. The other women cringed away from her as she walked towards the doorway. Fatima half expected her to turn around at the door to say something else, but she stepped out into the street and disappeared.

Part II

Thirteen

Nyamakeem inched slowly up the deserted street towards the sand dunes behind the village, the embers of the bonfire from the night before still emanating heat. The long shadows from the houses flanking either side of the street seemed to shrink away from her as she went. She walked slowly, leaning on a thick stick. The ascent made her legs hurt and her breathing laboured – she really was too old to do all this walking.

At the top of hill, she slowly turned around to observe the village spread out beneath her, down to the gardens and the river. The river was like a bit of string, following her through time and place, anchoring her here – to a village that she hated with all her heart – but also moving her along. She closed her eyes and the sounds and smells around her swiftly evaporated.

Nyamakeem opened her eyes again and it was dark. She had been told the villagers were early risers and early to bed, and as she moved down the narrow street the houses on either side of her were dark and silent, the only source of light the full moon shining between the grey clouds. The bundle she was carrying in her arms squirmed briefly then settled down, and she held it tightly with one hand while balancing herself with the other hand on the donkey she was riding. Her feet knocked against the animal's belly and the heavy bags hanging against its sides. It was 1943.

'Not too long now. It's that house with the black gates up ahead,' the man said. He held the donkey's reins in one hand and balanced a large carton box under his other arm; black honey and beeswax, brought all the way from the forests and plains of Malakal in the south to the dry dunes of the North. The rocking movement of the animal, the low light and the exhaustion of traveling for several days and nights all made Nyamakeem's eyelids heavier, and she fought to stay awake. She clutched the bundle tightly as it squirmed again. As they approached the high gates she saw that this house was different from the rest. Its walls were higher and built of slabs of stone, unlike the short mud walls of the other houses on either side of the street. And the gate had three planes, not two. The arch hanging over it was high up.

They stood in front of the gates now and Nyamakeem could see a faint light coming from within.

'My grandfather's lamp' Hassan said quietly, happily. He looked at the door for a long time, drinking in the black paint that he had clearly missed. He pushed his hand between two panels near the ground, his fingers searching for the handle to lift the anchor and override the lock. The gates swung open with a clang that rang out into the night air. Hassan stepped inside pulling the donkey with its riders behind him, and pushed the gates shut. Nyamakeem looked around her with apprehension. They were in a vast yard with high walls and a long veranda that ran the length of it. It was hard to make out the details in the dark, but she could see a faint white light flickering from within. She didn't have time to wonder, because at that minute they heard quick footsteps coming their way.

'Who goes there at this time of the night?' she heard a man bellow. The light approached them and soon a tall man stood in front of them, his sunken eyes jittering in the flickering light of the small flame.

'The same person who showed you how to open that gate from the outside without waking up Alhaj,' Hassan laughed, and stepped forward with his arms wide open. The man gasped.

'Hassan, my brother!'

'Abdal Wahab!'

The brothers embraced, laughing, slapping each other's shoulders and backs, pulling apart to look at each other's' faces and embracing again. Nyamakeem smiled at their happiness, and the apprehension she felt earlier slipped away. She looked down at the small sleeping face in her arms. Yes, it was like Hassan said. He definitely had their nose and forehead. She pulled her dress up slightly so that she could disembark and glanced up at Abdal Wahab, and her blood froze.

'What is this?' Abdal Wahab asked slowly, lifting the kerosene lamp and shining it into Nyamakeem's face. He stared at her and then down at the child she was carrying. Nyamakeem tried to smile, but the fierce eyes she was looking into made that difficult. She looked at Hassan hesitantly, who was still smiling, but his eyes were watchful.

'This is Nyamakeem, my wife. And that's my son.'

Abdal Wahab turned to stare at his brother in disbelief. 'Are you joking? This is your *wife*?'

'And my son. I named him Kheir Alseed, after our father.' He looked at his brother purposefully. Abdal Wahab looked back at Nyamakeem, and she felt her the hair on her skin stand up. She could barely understand what they were saying; her knowledge of Arabic was very little, and they had such a strange, thick accent.

'You named this Southerner's son after our father? This infidel?'

'She's no infidel, she's –'

'An animal worshipping infidel! Your so-called marriage isn't even valid! This child is a bastard! And you dare name him after our father?"

'What did you say?' Hassan said quietly, his eyes narrowing.

'I said this slave's son is a walad haram!'

It was like he had slapped Nyamakeem in the face. Slave? Did this man just call her a slave? That was a word she knew very well.

Hassan advanced on him, trembling with anger.

'Who are you calling a slave! That's my wife! She's the daughter of a chief!'

'Who or what she is does not concern me!' his brother roared, grabbing the front of Hassan's jallabiya. 'How dare you do such a thing! You'll make us a laughing stock of the village and all the villages around us! The son of Kheir Alseed Sidahmed, marrying a Southerner and having the gall to bring her to live among us as an equal! All the women in the family and the tribe weren't good enough for you? How dare you!'

Hassan grabbed Abdal Wahab's jallabiya and raised his fist to strike, but was stopped by a woman's voice.

'Hassan! My dear son!' the old woman cried out. She leaned against the wall, shuffling forward with difficulty. Hassan wrenched his brother's hand from his clothes and hurried over to greet her and kiss her hand. Hassan's mother kissed his forehead, held his face towards the light to look at him, tears streaming down his face.

'I feared your father and I would die before seeing you again! Look at how much weight you lost! Thanks to Allah you're finally home among your people!'

'Come and see what your son has brought home with him ya Hajja!'

Nyamakeem quivered in place, holding her son tightly to her chest. She wished she could fold in half and disappear. The darkness around them seemed to close in on her and her alone. Hassan's mother moved forward and peered at Nyamakeem in dismay.

'Oh Hassan, my son. What have you done?'

Hassan stiffened and pulled away from her.

'What he's done is that he's brought back a Southerner as his wife. He wants to humiliate us in front of everyone!'

'Yes, I married a Southerner. A Southerner worth a hundred Northern women!'

Hassan's mother stared at Nyamakeem in the low light, her wrinkled forehead scrunched up in confusion. Her eyes passed over the small bundle in her arms that Nyamakeem held close to her chest, her tears wetting the thin blanket. She put a withered hand over her mouth.

'Oh, Hassan. How could you bring her here?'

'We might as well bring all the servants out of their quarters and put them up in our rooms!'

'Ya Hajja,' Hassan said in a low voice, ignoring his brother. 'My son – our son – looks just like Aboy. Look at his face. I named him Kheir Alse-'

'Don't you say his name! He'll be sure to disown you when he sees what you've done!'

'Please! Please! What's done is done! My son is back with me after all these years, what does it matter the mistake that he made? It can all be rectified!'

Hassan spun around to face her.

'Mistake? Mistake? You're calling my marriage a mistake? I have the right to marry whoever I want!'

'You have the right to eat what you want and wear what you want, but you don't marry whoever or whatever you want. That's not your decision, its ours. It's the family's. You've brought shame on us!'

'My son, we are Arabs, Ashraaf,' his mother said, 'our lineage is pure and untainted and goes all the way back to the Prophet Mohamed peace be upon him. There is only Arab blood in it. Even your reckless relatives knew to keep their non-Arab adventures in the dark. That's the way it has always been. And that's the way it should always be.' She reached and held Hassan's face. 'Just take her away, let her go and come back to us! You're not the first one to take a black wife from the South, my son. But they all leave them there and start a family with someone proper. These people work for us. Up here we *own* them, you know that.'

Hassan jerked his face from her hands, grabbed the donkey's reigns and wrenched the animal around, almost dislodging Nyamakeem and the baby in her arms.

'Nyamakeem is my wife and this is my son, and if you don't accept that then I will have nothing more to do with you.'

He pulled the door open and dragged the donkey out, leaving his mother wailing behind him and his brother fuming.

'Don't you ever show your face in this house again!' he shouted, as the door slammed shut with a clang.

Nyamakeem was devastated. The shock wore off bit by bit, and as she bumped along on the donkey's brisk trot, she wept.

'Why did you bring me here? Didn't you know this was going to happen?'

Hassan looked back at her but did not reply. He pulled the donkey hurriedly through the silent streets.

'I know a place where we can spend the night there and see what the morning brings.'

He led them between the houses, over the dunes and towards the mountains. At the edge of the village the houses were visibly lifeless in the moonlight. Nyamakeem felt she was being watched as they got closer; there was something dark and alive about the mountains. The donkey voiced its discomfort as well, neighing and pulling at the reigns. The house Hassan led them to was nothing more than a shack. There was no light, no furniture. He emptied the carton and dumped its contents by the door, using the box first to sweep the floor then flattened it out and turned it into a bed for Nyamakeem to lie down on. He walked around the small yard turning rocks over with his shoe, stamping down on several scorpions that came scurrying out. Then he sat down heavily, his shoe next to him to keep watch for any unwelcome insects.

In the shade of the ominous mountain Nyamakeem lay down curled up with her back to Hassan, tears streaming down her face and onto the baby's cheeks as she breastfed him to sleep. The baby felt her agitation and whimpered, twisting his head away from her, then huddling back closer to the safety of her warm embrace. She cursed her decision to come to this place. She couldn't believe that she had even been looking forward to it, and Hassan had assured her many times that all would go well. How could he not have known how his family would react to their marriage? How could she – with everything that she knew – have believed that they would welcome her with open arms? She was no child, and it was no different where she came from, this rejection of the 'other'. But, she thought bitterly as she rocked the baby and tried to comfort him, she couldn't say she hadn't been warned.

And this strange land they had come to. It was so different to her home. There was sand everywhere, and the few scattered trees had provided little relief from the burning heat during their journey. The air was so dry it scraped against the back of her throat. It was nothing like the lush forests of the South and the vast plains of Malakal, where there were too many shades of green to count. There, it rained all year round, and the sand sucked up the moisture before the hour was up. The air was pure, the trees heavy with fruit that one just had to reach out and pick off. The milk was so plentiful they had to throw it out in the open so it wouldn't turn sour. And one could stand at the edge of any passing river, poke a sharp stick in and spear half a dozen fish with no effort at all. It was a world away from this arid desert. Why had she come here?

Both Hassan and Nyamakeem were awake when the sun came up the next day. They had a poor breakfast of the remaining dried bread and string cheese that they had been carrying with them on their journey to the village and a little water, then Hassan loaded their belongings back onto the donkey.

'We need to get back to the station in Karima, there might be a cargo train leaving tomorrow.'

They made their way back through the ruins, making a wide circle around the houses, and crossed over the sand dunes behind the village heading back north. Their progress was slow, impeded by the rising sun with its impossible heat. The scenery was a monotonous desert broken only by a large, grand mountain standing all alone with what looked like statues in its shade. It looked nothing like the dark mountains they had slept beneath the night before. They passed several villages, only stopping in one of them to find water and fresh bread, then continued their journey towards Karima which they reached in the early evening. Hassan guided the donkey straight to the station, stood it outside and crossed the platform to find information about the outgoing trains to Khartoum. The passenger train came and left once a week – they had arrived on it yesterday morning and it had left in the afternoon. There was a cargo train expected tomorrow morning. Some coaxing and exchange of money secured Hassan and Nyamakeem's place in one of the cars.

Hassan found the porter whose donkey they had rented the previous night. If he was surprised to see them so soon he didn't show it, and watched them as they removed their belongings from the animal in order to give it back to him.

'Back to Khartoum in the morning?' he asked Hassan.

'Yes, if Allah wills it.' Hassan did not provide an explanation and expected the man to question him further. Instead he offered them boarding for the night.

'And that baby looks like he could use some high-quality goat milk.'

They did not need to be asked twice. Their breakfast the next morning was much fancier: hot fava beans with fennel and sesame oil, fresh eggs, and sweet tea with milk and gargosh. The porter's wife and her children played with the baby while Nyamakeem dipped the strange, hard biscuits into the tea, trying to soften them, feeling a little better than the day before. By midmorning they were seated in the corner of the train car surrounded by huge sacks of coal. There were a few other passengers, all stashed away in different cars in the same unofficial manner. It was a very different trip from the one they had taken on the comfortable Karima train two days before, where Hassan had booked them a first-class cabin that they had had to themselves. The screeching wheels and whistles of the conductor signalled the beginning of their trip and once again they plunged into the desert, this time headed back to Khartoum.

Nyamakeem disembarked the next morning, her legs stiff and her ears ringing from the long sit on the noisy train and followed Hassan through the crowd of workers and merchants clamouring. They emerged from the train station and stood by the side of the road. Men and women called to them from their stalls and mats on the pavement near the station's entrance, inviting them to buy their merchandise.

Hassan left Nyamakeem and the baby in the shade of a Neem tree and disappeared for over two hours. People passing by looked curiously at the pair, and Nyamakeem returned their stares with the same sentiment. She had never seen so many Northerners and Arabs in one place before.

They talked to her and about her. She could understand a little of what they were saying but did not respond. She was homesick and exhausted. Every bone in her body ached and she was constantly on the verge of tears. Finally, Hassan returned, carrying a box of vegetables and bread, and a key. Behind him was a young boy pulling a donkey cart.

With their meagre belongings, they rode on the cart and headed to El Sajana, a sprawling neighbourhood flanking the El Sajana market. Hassan directed the boy deeper and deeper until they came to a house on the outskirts of the neighbourhood. A short, portly women was leaning against the front door and watched the family with interest as they disembarked.

'This is your wife?' she asked, looking Nyamakeem up and down. Nyamakeem stared back at her, ready to swipe out if she heard the word 'slave' again. Instead, the woman reached out and pinched Kheir Alseed's cheek, giving him a wet kiss.

'You're on that side,' she said, pointing to a small metal door down the wall, then turned around and stepped back into her house. It was more of a room than a house, with a door that didn't close all the way, and they could hear their landlords clearly through the wall that separated them. There was no yard or alley. The room like the rest of the house was built from mud bricks with two small openings near the roof to let in air and light. In the corner was a tiny cooking area, and in the other corner was the small clay zeer, the water inside it cooled by the breeze coming from the high windows. But it was a place to call their own. Only after they had settled in that night, squashed together on the narrow rope bed that was the only piece of furniture in the room, did Hassan talk about their unpleasant encounter.

'I'm sorry.'

Nyamakeem rubbed Kheir Alseed's back and kept his legs curled under him as he lay face first on her tummy, trying to ease the colic that had been plaguing him for the past week. She did not respond.

'I should have known this would happen. I thought that things would have changed in all these years that I was away, that our family bond was closer than anything else. I was wrong.'

Kheir Alseed let out a large belch and Nyamakeem fought to keep her laughter down. She was still angry and hurt and didn't want this moment to pass lightly. Since when did prejudice melt into nothing in a few years? Hassan was either disillusioned or simple.

'In all cases, this doesn't change anything. We came here because we wanted to build a life together for our son. It's actually better that we try to do that away from our families. Here in Khartoum, we can give him the best opportunities. He will have the best life.'

Then, more to himself than to her: 'All these years away and the village looked just the same. Like I had never left.'

Nyamakeem turned her face to the wall and closed her eyes.

Little by little, they made the house a home, and Nyamakeem pushed the horror of her encounter with her in-laws to the back of her mind. With his savings, Hassan set up a small stall in the El Sajana market selling vegetables that he bought from the local farmers. Their first real purchase was a donkey and cart so that he could transport the produce from the farms to the market early in the morning. Bit by bit, they populated the small room, adding some low stools, another roped bed, dishes and cookware, and a metal trunk for storage. They settled down into a routine, though not to Nyamakeem's liking.

There was nothing for her to do in Khartoum. She had no friends, no one to talk to other than Hassan, and nothing much to talk about except his day and random bits of news that he had heard. She couldn't communicate with her neighbours and they quickly lost interest in trying to decipher her signing. The newspapers Hassan sometimes brought back home were in Arabic, and she had to have him read to her so she could know what was going on in the world outside their small dwelling. It surprised her how little news from the South there was; as if it was a separate country. With a one-year-old baby and household chores she didn't have much time to herself, but it was very different from the life she had led in the South.

Back home, her life in a Shilluk village in Malakal had been anything but idle. Life had orientated around a hut with the thatched roof, her family's gol. From a young age she had followed her mother and older sisters around as they worked in the maize and millet gardens, cooked in the hut in the back of their plot and fashioned cooking utensils, while her brothers and father herded the cattle, spear fished in the White Nile and hunted hippopotamus, antelope, buffalo and giraffes. Her father was the headsman leading their pac; the hamlet formed by their gol, and those of several other extended families'. Grouped together with other clans' hamlets, they formed settlements that were strung along the White Nile like beads on a string, each settlement under a chief approved by the divine king, or reth, who ruled over the Shilluk from his palace in Fashoda.

Each hamlet would keep their cattle together in one place. Every night Nyamakeem would watch the dancing shadows of the cows tied around a dung fire to keep away the insects, imagining them singing and jumping in their own celebration of life, or taking part in a great battle. Her days were full and satisfying, surrounded by the warmth of her family and the familiarity and protection of the clan. Their routine, unbroken since birth, until her father decided that Nyamakeem and her brothers would go to the mission school.

She still remembered the day she turned seven and her father had called her into the yard and told her. She had been bemused and couldn't understand why none of her cousins or friends were going, but her father was not one to wait for a child's approval of his decisions. The subgrade school, which was just a cleared ground under a tree, was a short walk from her house. It had around twenty boys and three girls at first, but as they progressed the students dropped out one by one until only Nyamakeem and a dozen boys were left. Her work in the gardens and kitchen was now substituted by learning how to read and copy the Bible in her Shilluk language. She was still allowed to help around the house after school and so was kept busy all day, and the two years of subgrade school passed by quickly, at the end of which she passed her exams easily and was offered a place in the American Presbyterian Mission's Doleib Hill elementary school for girls in Meridi. She refused, of course, as it was a boarding school two whole day's trek from her village where she would have to live all year. But her father had other plans.

Standing at the crooked door that wouldn't close all the way, Kheir Alseed on her hip watching the passersby happily, these memories of Nyamakeem's home felt like memories from another lifetime she had lived. She still felt like that little girl catching the raindrops bouncing off the thatched roof in her mouth during the day, and watching the dancing shadows of the cows at night. The child who sat by the riverbank watching her brothers plunge their sharp spears into the water, easily catching the slippery silver fish and flick them over their shoulders into their baskets. She remembered her father's conniption when the village elders had decreed that he was to pay the price of one ox for her brother's foolishness with one of the girls in the settlement; as the head of the family, he was the one who took responsibility for any offenses committed by them. It had been all the more embarrassing for him being the headsman of the hamlet. Kheir Alseed broke out into laughter and pulled at her sleeve excitedly, and Nyamakeem came out of her reverie to see Hassan coming home. She smiled; this was her favourite part of the day, seeing his familiar face emerge from the crowd. But, she wondered, it was still too early for him to be returning. It seemed that something was wrong. Rather than his laughing embrace, Hassan walked slowly towards them looking down, his face ashen.

'My father is dead.'

Fourteen

They sat in silence in the small room, Hassan on the ground leaning against the wall and hugging himself, still holding the telegram that had brought him the painful news. He looked like a small boy. Nyamakeem watched him sadly and recalled how excited he had been to return to the North after all those years in the South. He had told her so much about his family that she felt she knew them up close. He had dozens of stories about his father in particular: how as a child he had ridden behind him on his donkey and smelled his cologne, how he climbed onto his back when he knelt for prayer. How his father had prayed over him all night when Hassan had fallen out of three-metre high date tree and almost died. As soon as they knew she was pregnant, Hassan had told her that if the baby was a boy he wanted to name him Kheir Alseed, after his father. He could not get over the way they had parted without seeing him and that he had died without reconciling.

'It's all Abdal Wahab's fault. That animal!'

He would travel north to see his family and visit his father's grave.

Nyamakeem watched him with worry as he packed a small bag of belongings and counted out some money for her until his return. Kheir Alseed tottered around him, pulling clothes out of the bag and hanging onto his neck.

'Will you come back?'

He looked up at her in surprise.

'Of course I'll come back,' he said, tying a bit of rope around his old bag. 'And while I'm there I might as well see about my inheritance. Whether or not they agree with my choices is one thing; they can't deny me my rights, and it's better to do this sooner than later. I want to have things in order for our son.'

At dawn Hassan stood by the open door, his bag under his arm and his turban thrown over his shoulder. He looked very different from when they had first met all those years ago. He was younger then of course, his soft shiny hair a dark black, and the vertical shulookh scars on his face clear and dark. He had always been smiling: that was the thing Nyamakeem remembered the most, and the first thing she had noticed when they had first met: this strange looking man who was smiling at her. Even though he had been wrapped up in white gauze and in obvious pain, he had smiled at her through the open window of his hospital room that looked out onto the yard where she had stood with Alek one sunny afternoon.

The man in front of Nyamakeem now looked as if he had aged twenty years since then: his thinning hair was patched with grey, and the shulookh scars were barely visible with his sun burnt cheeks. His aging jallabiya was yellowed and patched where she had repeatedly mended the holes. It was probably better for him to see his family and make amends with them. God knew she would do anything to be with her own family again.

'This is my home,' he told her, and kissed her forehead.

'This is where I'll always come back to. As long as I live, my home is with you.'

When Hassan walked out and pulled the door shut behind him, Nyamakeem felt as if a candle had been blown at and she was left in darkness. It didn't take long for the immensity of her loneliness to descend on her. She cried as she put Kheir Alseed down for his nap and lay down next to him, not just because she missed Hassan already, but because of the reality of being completely dependent on him even for companionship. She still felt like a fish out of water in the North.

In his absence, Nyamakeem waited for as long as she could before venturing out to replenish their stock of food. Hassan had left in such a hurry he had not had time to leave them enough until he returned. When there was nothing left after four days, she took a fistful of coins, wrapped her lawa in a knot over her right shoulder and stepped out of the house with Kheir Alseed perched on her hip. She had only ventured along the closest streets to their house before and hadn't dared go into the big market, so she walked towards the main road where she knew there would be some small stalls.

'Five piasters,' the man sitting on the mat told the woman in front of her when she pointed at the mound of tomatoes sitting next to him. Nyamakeem realised she had no idea how much things cost, if this was a good price or a bad one. She wasn't even sure what the man was charging the five piasters for: a dozen tomatoes? Half a dozen? She waited and watched as the pair argued and the man counted out five tomatoes for the woman which she put into a weaved basket she was holding then handed him the money.

Without saying anything, Nyamakeem stepped forward, pointed to the tomatoes and brandished her five piasters in the man's face. He sat cross-legged on the mat, chewing his tobacco and looking up at her and Kheir Alseed. Then he let out a stream of brown-tinged spit through his teeth, reached out and took the money and counted out four tomatoes. Nyamakeem did not argue, not only because she didn't know how to convey her irritation in a language this man could understand, but because she had forgotten her basket at home and had to fit everything in her hands and lawa. When she arrived home, she deposited the baby and the produce on the metal table that served as a counter and storage area. There was one thought in her head: she had to learn Arabic.

Hassan returned one month later – a month that felt like a year – and Nyamakeem wept with both happiness and relief. The family reunion had been a difficult one. Hassan had refused to reconcile with his brother unless the family acknowledged his marriage and rescinded their insults, which they had no intention of doing. But when he was getting ready to return home, his mother had reluctantly conceded on the condition that Nyamakeem and her son stay in Khartoum and their existence remain an absolute secret.

Nyamakeem waited to hear what the rest of the condition for reconciliation was, but Hassan said no more. She did not press him. But she sensed he was holding back on something. Despite his disappointment, the trip back home appeared to have done him good: he looked well-fed and more relaxed than he had for a long time. Judging by the size of the house she had seen, the obvious wealth, and her basic knowledge of how the Arabs honoured their guests in all their occasions, she guessed that many sheep had been slaughtered during the funeral and that Hassan had enjoyed several well-rounded meals for a change. She did not begrudge him that; she was just happy for his return.

'There is also good news,' Hassan said. 'Haj Alhadi died.'

'What do you mean "good news"? Who is Haj Alhadi?' Nyamakeem asked in surprise. Hassan laughed.

'Haj Alhadi – may Allah have mercy on him – was my father's youngest brother. I don't mean I'm happy that he's dead. We didn't really know him that well; he had been away in Marrakesh his entire adult life, at the Ben Yousif Madrassa. I didn't even know he had returned to Sudan. I was told that he only appeared a year ago, at death's door; some sort of wasting illness that he had been suffering from. At the end of his life he wanted to be buried near his family. The good news is that he never married and has no children, and died just ten days before my father, may Allah have mercy on both their souls. And since my father was the only living brother, he inherited everything from him, and now that inheritance has come to us.'

Haj Alhadi had brought back with him most of the wealth he had accumulated over the years after leaving behind two buildings donated as dormitories for students at the Madrassa, and an orphanage. He also had a considerable share of the family's date gardens and other assets they had inherited from their father. Muslims had complicated inheritance customs that were laid out in the Quran, Hassan explained as he bounced Kheir Alseed on his knee, with the recipients' shares conditional on when the deceased had passed away, if they were married or not, had sons, daughters, living parents, or siblings, and if the recipient was a male or female. It became even more complicated when families waited for long periods to divide the inheritance and other people died in the middle. So when someone like Hassan's uncle died and had neither spouse nor child nor living parent, the division was somewhat straight forward: the living sibling inherited everything.

'Our son will have a good life,' Hassan said happily.

Nyamakeem listened with wonder and tried to wrap her head around the numbers and calculations Hassan forecasted. It was so much money. And it was like Hassan had said: the family could not deny him his right to the inheritance, especially since the whole village knew about it. But for the time being, they still had very little. They had gone through most of Hassan's savings and his work in the market was barely enough to pay their rent and provide for two modest meals a day, with meat twice a week. Nyamakeem did her best to stretch their supplies of sorghum flour, fava beans and dried okra to cover the whole week, so any additional income was more than welcome.

It was so drudging, this necessity of money in exchange for anything at all. Nyamakeem remembered a time when her people paid for everything in kind; even taxes to the British government. Their activity was for subsistence only: they grew and hunted enough to feed them. There was little sense of insecurity, no need to save or accumulate wealth. It was the missionaries who had introduced this work-for-money concept, paying those of them who worked on the mission first with beads, wire and cloth, then in money: three piasters for a full day at work.

'So how did you manage while I was away?'

'We need to talk about that,' Nyamakeem said resolutely. And so they began her Arabic lessons, an hour in the evenings after Kheir Alseed had gone to sleep. Sometimes Nyamakeem felt like she was back under the shade of the moringa tree, painstakingly writing her Bible verses as the teacher droned on over their heads. To make learning easier, Hassan spoke with her in Arabic at home instead of Shilluk, which was for both for her and Kheir Alseed's benefits now that he was picking up words. When Nyamakeem knocked on their landlord's door one day and used her broken Arabic to ask for some salt, the woman smiled, and Nyamakeem smiled back.

Three months later, Hassan came home early again. This time, the family had sent word with the incoming lorries that his mother was sick and wished to see him. He still hadn't gotten over not seeing his father before his passing and was almost in a panic. He would travel to the village and stay with her for a couple of months. He could also take that opportunity to clear up whatever procedures related to the inheritance remained. He wanted to make sure that Nyamakeem and Kheir Alseed's affairs were in order in case anything happened to him.

Nyamakeem looked at Hassan as he stood in the doorway at dawn, the familiar worry gnawing at her. Kheir Alseed was confidently walking now and Hassan picked him up, kissed him and held him tight. He looked at Nyamakeem over the baby's head.

'I'll be back before you know it.'

It felt to Nyamakeem as if he was reassuring himself more than her. She felt the room closing in on her again as the door swung shut behind him. He was leaving them behind again. Her loneliness crept up on her from the corners of the room that was still dark. She watched Kheir Alseed as he banged on the door, calling for his father, and let out a heavy sigh.

This time, Hassan stayed for almost three months. Nyamakeem, now more familiar with life in Khartoum on their own and armed with the local language, left the house almost every day. She could barter a little with the sellers now and spaced out her purchasing so that she could buy something different every time. Twice, she ventured further away from the house towards the train station. She still had no friends, but she expected this would change: the condominium rule had reversed the Southern Policy that had virtually cut the country in two. For the first time, Nyamakeem saw Southerners – tired and dusty – disembarking from the trains.

In the year that she had lived in Khartoum, Nyamakeem had seen very few Southerners, except for a few soldiers retired from the Egyptian army who now lived on the far end of El Diyoum. The British government had not wanted the Arab Muslims infiltrating the South, corrupting the people and spreading their despised 'Mohamedanism' into the rest of Africa. So, they had enacted a closed territory policy in the South, replacing Arab infantry in the military with the Equatorian Corps, relocating all Northern Sudanese administrators to the North and pushing out Northern merchants. Only those with a permit were allowed to enter and stay in the South with the assurance that they were there only for commercial purposes with no intention of preaching their Muslim religion. Hassan had been one such person, and that's why it had been a surprise for Nyamakeem to see him in Doleib Hill when virtually all Northerners had been expelled for many years. In fact, he had been the first Northerner she had ever seen up close.

Coming to Doleib Hill elementary school had been against her will. She resisted as loudly as she could, but she was no match for her father and could not understand his insistence on her education even when he had explained it to her.

'The best way to beat your enemy is to learn their language.'

The Shilluk people – proud, powerful warriors and raiders their entire lives with a kingdom that had once reigned all the way to the confluence of the White and Blue Niles in the north – had never overcome their defeat and subjugation by the British. The tribes of the South had put up a gallant resistance to occupation, but in the end spears and canoes were no match for fire power and steamers. They remained hostile to the invaders, their animosity and mistrust compounded by the raging slave trade that was at first run by the Turkish government, then to which the British turned a blind eye when it was supposed to have been abolished.

And so Nyamakeem found herself deposited in the Doleib Hill boarding school for girls, away from her family and pac for the first time. The whole place was strange and new to her: while her teacher in the village school had been a young Chollo man who taught them in their own language and dialect, the teachers here were white-skinned nuns who spoke English and an array of Nilotic languages. The work was so much more difficult; arithmancy, English, Christian studies and sewing. They were reprimanded constantly and not allowed an hour of idleness. Nyamakeem hated it and more than once thought of escape. But she had no idea how to get back home and was fearful of facing her father's wrath should she be successful. And then she made a friend – a Dinka girl by the name of Alek – and life became more tolerable at the school. She was even happy to return the year after, and the year after that. When the four years were drawing to an end, the nuns asked her if she would be interested in teaching at one of the new schools in her village. A teacher? Nyamakeem had never considered such a thing.

'I think you would make a great teacher,' Alek told her as they walked side by side under the shadows of the palm trees. 'It's better than going back and doing nothing after everything you've learned here.'

While boys had the option of going to secondary schools in Juba and Uganda, and training to be clerks, carpenters and tailors, girls had no such opportunities. They were such a small percentage of students that it wasn't deemed worth the expenses. The majority of Southern tribes still saw no need to send their daughters to the missionary schools. Despite her initial hatred of the school, Nyamakeem could see the attraction in a teaching position, especially since she would be the first and only girl in her village to be one. The years at boarding school and the change in routine had removed her from her family life; the life she had known nothing other than before. When she went home during the holidays she still helped in the gardens and the kitchen, but she no longer saw the dancing and battling shadows of the cows in the firelight. She just saw shadows.

Nyamakeem and Alek had circled the mission and crossed the long yard, coming up to the small hospital building. This was Nyamakeem's favourite place and she came here whenever she could. They watched the missionary nurses bustling in and out of the wards, talking to the only elderly doctor, bossing the patients back into their beds. Through the windows Nyamakeem could see them placing equipment in boiling water. She knew the needle with the sharp tip was used to administer their medicines. She admired the starched, white uniforms they wore and the serious looks on their faces.

'Don't look now, but there's a strange-looking man staring at you. I think he's a Northerner.'

In her surprise Nyamakeem turned and looked directly where she had been told not to, drawing an exasperated 'tsk!' from Alek. Sure enough, looking at them out of one of the windows was a light-skinned man with markings on his cheeks. He was smiling at them – at her. Nyamakeem stared back at him in curiosity. He looked as if he had been trodden on by a water buffalo; his head was bandaged, he had a black eye and his arm was tied up in a bit of cloth. Then he spoke to them.

'Good morning!'

It was actually late afternoon, and hearing his broken Chollo and mispronunciation half-shouted at them across the yard made both girls laugh. They ventured closer to the building.

'What's your name?' Nyamakeem asked. The man answered directly; he appeared to be used to this question.

'Hassan.'

'Assa?' Alek repeated the strange name with a laugh. The man laughed with her.

'H-assa-nnn,' he corrected.

'Ha-san,' Nyamakeem said. A strange name for a strange man.

'The school?' the man asked, leaning on the window with a wince and nodding his head in the direction of the school.

'Yes, we're from the school. Where are you from?'

He said something that sounded like shshh which they couldn't understand. He sensed their confusion and stated the obvious: 'from up North.' He told them that he had been in Malakal for two years, and in Wau four years before then. He recognised Alek as a Dinka and asked her where her family was from, Dinka Bor? Dinka Agak? Nyamakeem sensed that he was showing off his knowledge of the South. His Dinka was much better than his Shilluk, though the latter was not that bad.

A nurse appeared behind Hassan carrying a tray with the needle which Hassan looked at with horror. She glared at the girls through the window and dismissed them back to the school. Hassan called out after them to come back tomorrow.

Nyamakeem thought about Alek as she watched the tall, elderly Dinka man standing at the entrance to the train station with a small bag under his arm. It had been almost seven years since she had last seen her friend. Once their studies at Doleib Hill were over, Alek had moved back to Renk to be married. There had been no way to keep in touch. The old man was dressed in ill-fitting trousers, a faded shirt and a pair of snakeskin markoub. He was soon joined by a younger man and a woman who were also dressed strangely, as if unused to this attire; the woman wore a long-sleeved dress with the traditional lawa tied in a knot over her right shoulder. They looked around the area in apparent confusion, talking among themselves and pointing in different directions. Then they moved towards the market. The woman scanned the crowd as they walked and her eyes fell on Nyamakeem standing a distance away. She stopped and her eyes opened in surprise, and she made to reach out to the young man. But then her eyes flitted up to Nyamakeem's forehead, looked down at the light skinned child in her arms, and her initial expression of delight was replaced by something nearer repulsion. She turned her face away and followed the men.

Nyamakeem was disappointed but not very surprised: the Dinka woman had recognised the scarring on her forehead and identified her as a Shilluk. But while there were known historical animosities between the Dinka and the Nuer tribes, there was little trouble between the Dinka and Shilluk, and their languages were somewhat similar. Nyamakeem sensed the woman's disgust was not because of where she was evidently from, but because of the half-cast child in her arms. Nyamakeem looked wistfully after the trio feeling like she had just caught – and lost – a whiff of the cool, clear air of her childhood in the middle of that hot, dusty market. But no matter; there would be others coming now. There would be others coming.

Fifteen

When Hassan walked through the door late one evening, he was covered in mud and smiling broadly. He had left for the village in early summer and it was now late autumn, and Khartoum had transformed into one big muddy swamp. Nyamakeem leaped into his arms but Kheir Alseed cowered behind the bed; he didn't recognise the man reaching out to him, and only after coaxing and bribing with some sweet dates did the boy hesitantly allow his father to hold him.

Hassan's face was round and shiny, his jallabiya a bright white, and the once-permanent smile had returned to his lips. He was full of laughter and good news and eager to share it. His mother's health had improved and he had made amends with his family. They had worked out all the assets: the shops, the houses, plots of date gardens, mango gardens, citrus gardens, empty pieces of land, and the endless heads of livestock. Hassan had set up the fund and made the arrangements to have the money sent quarterly to him in Khartoum. Their luck was finally changing.

True enough, with the funds Hassan had brought with him they moved out of the tiny room into a small one-bedroom house with its own entrance and a small yard. There was now meat, chicken or fish on the lunch tray every day. Hassan threw out all his old, ragged jallabiyas and was once again dressed in white splendour. When the second payment arrived three months later, he bought Nyamakeem a large silver nose ring. He hired a young man to manage the vegetable stall and opened a small shop in the El Sajana market where he sold dates, tobacco and dried spices delivered to him from the village. Both his financial and social capital improved with this move, and he soon hired another boy to help him with the customers.

However, unlike other merchants, he never brought his own son to his shop, just like he never went out with Nyamakeem in public. He didn't even take Kheir Alseed to Friday prayers with him. The house they had moved into, while of better quality, was even further away from his workplace than their first room. Hassan had to take two different buses to get to his shop, and as a result he left the house before the sun was up and only came home in the late evening. Nyamakeem understood why things were this way, but her initial nonchalance gradually grew teeth and transformed into resentment. She did not complain but did not bother to hide her irritation either. The looks she sometimes drew when she walked the streets with Kheir Alseed were full of scorn; to the outside world, Nyamakeem was the single Southern mother of an Arab child. For all anyone knew, the child could have been born from some random Arab's adventure, and both him and his mother discarded afterwards. And sometimes that was what it felt like.

'Kheir Alseed should start school soon,' Hassan said one evening as he lay on his side drinking his black tea after a late lunch. Kheir Alseed was walking around wearing Hassan's markoub on his feet and singing a Chollo folk song with half the words made up. The shoes were too big and he kept tripping over. Nyamakeem washed the pot and tray from lunch and put them against the wall to dry, tipped the dishwater out of the large steel basin into the alley and leaned that next to the cookware. Hassan continued, not waiting for her response.

'There is the Quaranic school run by Elfaki Mahmoud. He could start there, but I think he should progress directly to the new elementary school in El Diyoum. If our son is to be an afandi like we wished, he needs to start right.'

'And who is going to drop him off and pick him up from this school, I wonder?'

Hassan sipped his tea slowly, keeping his eyes on Kheir Alseed. He took his time to answer.

'You could take him. It's quite a distance, but it wouldn't take too much of your time.'

She could almost hear the rest of the sentence in his head: it's not like you have anything important to do with your time anyway. She felt her blood boil but took a deep breath.

'I'm happy to take him and bring him back. But they will need to know who his father is. Who my *husband* is.'

Hassan paused, still avoiding looking at her. Then he slowly drained his cup and set it down on the ground next to the bed. He spoke calmly, as if rehearsed.

'Āmaarø, my sweetheart. I know our situation is not ideal, but you remember what my family's condition was. We can't let our marriage be known to anyone. I can't risk anyone from the village seeing us together or finding out about you and Kheir Alseed. It would be deeply embarrassing for my family and catastrophic for my relationship with them.'

He finally met her eye.

'Believe me, there is nothing I want more than to enjoy my marriage in public. I wish I could bring you both back to the village with me. I wish we could all live there together. But,' he hesitated, and once again averted his gaze, 'but even if my family did accept our marriage, you still wouldn't be comfortable there. The rest of the village shares the same sentiment – the whole area, in fact. Even if we won my family over, we would still be up against the rest of the world.'

He looked at Nyamakeem who glared back at him, her anger pulsating. It was at moments of helpless fury like these that she felt the most trapped; that the house she was in, the city she was in, was nothing more than a prison, an exile. She cursed her decision to follow Hassan to the North and her own naivety. They had come here to give their son a better life. She and Hassan had discussed their and their son's future endlessly, always reaching the same conclusion: if Kheir Alseed was to have an education and a career after that, it had to be in Khartoum. The North had five times as many schools, its economy was flourishing and it even had a college now. It was so easy to get from one place to another with the roads and trams, unlike the dense forest and unfriendly Sudd which cut people off for months back home. Kheir Alseed could choose to be anything he wanted here: a government employee, a teacher, even a doctor. He had none of those options in the South. There wasn't even a railway; when they had travelled north they had had to take the steamer all the way to Kosti where they got on the train to Khartoum and from there to Karima. The development and infrastructure in the South were so far behind anything in the North, and it was obvious the Condominium Rule had no plans to change this.

Nyamakeem knew all of this. And she had known it wouldn't be easy for her if she agreed to leave the South, but she had never imagined it would this hard, this humiliating. It was true that she had come here for her son; but she also come to be with Hassan, for them all to be a family. Nyamakeem knew that this was the only way for them to go forward. But at what cost?

When Hassan came home early again, Nyamakeem knew what he was going to say before he said it. This time his nephew was getting married and he was expected at the wedding. He also wished to spend some time with his mother and had to make arrangements for larger deliveries of stock for his shop now that he was expanding his business. He packed much larger bags this time with presents for the family and supplies for the wedding. A whole suitcase was dedicated just to the cloth: imported white Swiss voile to be divided among the men of the family and the groom, and colourful tiyab – also imported Swiss – with silk embroidery for the women. Another bag was filled with perfumes, leather sandals, handbags and imported cigarettes. And now that he had Ibrahim minding the stall and two boys managing the shop in his absence, he would be gone for longer.

'I understand,' Nyamakeem said. And she did. She understood that this was how the rest of their life was going to be. Hassan would have two families, would lead two lives separate from each other. He would enjoy his big, wealthy family in his village where he belonged, and come back to his secret family in Khartoum. She would always be the one left behind. But, she comforted herself, she would also be the one he came back to.

It was Nyamakeem's oldest sister's wedding that she remembered the most. It hadn't been the first in their pac, but it was certainly the most glamorous. The groom was the son of the headsman of a settlement north from theirs and had met her sister at another wedding. Nyagine was well known in the area for her beautiful almond shaped eyes, and Nyamakeem was flattered when told that she looked so much like her. The groom presented a sheep in their gol yard as a first step. When Nyamakeem's father accepted the sheep, this signalled the beginning of the ceremony: the 'tyeengi møgø' or brewing of the beer, and the exciting 'møgø thike', the wedding dance, and once the bride wealth had been accepted, the wedding feast. The groom had presented an impressive number of cattle, far above the minimum of ten heads: twenty cows and a bull, fifty sheep and goats, and spears and shields for Nyamakeem's father. The Shilluk owned nowhere near the number of cattle that the Dinka and Nuer did, but they were still their pride and measure of wealth.

When Hassan had proposed to Nyamakeem under the shade of the trees in the hospital yard, she wondered first if he could afford even ten heads of cattle for her dowry. Hassan had managed to remain in the South despite the Southern Policy, but his business had suffered. Whether or not she should accept his proposal came second, and how her father would react to this news trailed closely behind.

There was no love lost between the Shilluk and the Northerners. She had told no one that she was seeing Hassan, or that the main reason she had accepted the teaching position was so that she could stay longer in the Doleib Hill for training so that they could meet. She had not got as far as the expectation that he would ask her to marry him.

'Don't you have any cousins up there?' she teased.

'I had a hundred cousins and there are probably a hundred more now. I've been away for so long I lost touch.'

'And if I say yes? What next?'

'Then I get the sheep.'

Nyamakeem laughed.

'You know what I mean. What next? Will I move into your gol? Do you even have one? Where do you even live?' Nyamakeem realised she knew very little about Hassan.

'I can build one in your settlement if that's what you like. You will need to be near your family anyway when the baby comes.'

'The baby! You really have thought this through.'

'It's all I've been thinking about these past two months.'

Nyamakeem had laughed. Then, seeing the serious expression on his face, looked away demurely.

∾

The woman behind the desk looked at Nyamakeem, her expression blank behind her glasses.

'You're this boy's mother, you say?'

Nyamakeem adjusted her tob – which had replaced the traditional lawa of the South but which she still wore thrown over her right shoulder – and pulled Kheir Alseed away from the door again. He fidgeted and fussed as she stood him in front of the desk so the woman could see him. Then he wriggled away and ran back to the door to look out at the yard which was full of boys running around and shouting on their break.

'His name is Kheir Alseed. Yes, I'm his mother.'

'And where is his father? He should be the one to register the child.'

'He works long hours at the market, and in any case is traveling now.'

Nyamakeem stared the school headmistress squarely in the eye, almost daring her to push back. The woman leaned back in her seat and examined the pair with interest. Nyamakeem had taken extra care with their appearance that morning: they wore their best clothes, the new markoub Hassan had bought Kheir Alseed, her silver nose ring and a collection of earrings. She kept her new snakeskin handbag visible at her chest and shook her bangles with every movement. I was a teacher once too, you know, she wanted to tell the headmistress. In a place far away from here, in a language very different from yours, with children who looked very different from the ones playing in the school yard out there. But it was still teaching.

The school was one of the best in Khartoum and did not grant admission to just anyone. The administration was known for their preference for sons of big families, wealthy merchants and religious figures. More than half of its graduates entered Gordon's College, while the others took on their families' businesses or went to Egypt and Morocco for religious training. There were no Southerners in the school. But as Hassan had reminded her with confidence, Kheir Alseed was from the North.

The headmistress finished her inspection and leaned forward again, picking up a pen. Nyamakeem held her breath.

'He starts Saturday.'

Kheir Alseed was not the only one growing: the city around them was changing rapidly and its population was swelling. Its inhabitants were also changing. As Nyamakeem predicted, more and more Southerners were arriving; passing through Khartoum to get to other places, or settling to stay. With Kheir Alseed in school and more time on her hands, Nyamakeem continued to pass by the train station where she stood around for up to an hour sometimes, waiting to see if a familiar face would appear. Often, the sight of her drew a smile from the arrivals, and sometimes a scowl. Towering over the crowd she was hard to miss. Nyamakeem knew enough about the city by now to provide some guidance to the new arrivals. They did not always know each other's dialect and often resorted to pidgin Arabic, or Arabi Juba to communicate. That was how she met James and Zereda, a young Azande couple from Yambio who were coming to the North for the first time.

They had already disembarked when Nyamakeem arrived and saw her before she saw them. She had put her weaved basket of vegetables on the ground and looked up to see them standing over her, smiling broadly.

'A Chollo sister! What a lovely welcome after such a long journey.'

Nyamakeem laughed in pleasant surprise and reached out to shake their hands, but the woman hugged her tightly instead. Zereda, as she introduced herself, had an easy smile and a sense of adventure. Her full tummy pressed against Nyamakeem's as they embraced; she was six months pregnant. The pair reminded Nyamakeem of herself when she arrived in the North with Hassan.

'Dawire, sister, are you ok?' James asked. Nyamakeem shut her eyes tightly and opened them again, banishing the dark echo from the past and forcing herself into the daylight. She smiled broadly at them and invited them to her house. Having nowhere else to go and being exhausted from the long ride, they readily agreed. On the bus, Nyamakeem watched their faces as they stared out of the window at the streets and people passing by outside, and was once again drawn back to her first days in the North. How optimistic she had been, how much she had been looking forward to her new life with Hassan. Had it really been only five years?

'How was your journey? Did you come on the steamboats through Kosti as well?' Nyamakeem asked as she washed the spinach and tomatoes for their late breakfast. She sat on a low stool near the open door so she could speak with the guests inside while working in her small kitchen, a shaded corner of the yard with a small coal burner, a bucket of water and a table with utensils and plates. Zereda rubbed her swollen ankles as she reclined on a bed in the small living room and James sat between her and the door.

'Yes, that's correct. We travelled to Taufikia with the caravans and got on the steamer from there, stopped for a week at Kosti. Then we took the railroad through Medani to Khartoum. This railroad, they told us it crosses the whole country from east to west. I've never seen anything like it! It's as if the forces colonising the North are not the same ones colonising the South.'

Nyamakeem chopped the spinach and tomatoes and put them aside. The small coal burner in the corner was hot now and she put the beef cubes in the small pan to brown, added the peanut sauce then the chopped vegetables. The aroma made all three of their stomachs grumble hungrily.

'Since we got off the steamer, it feels like we've entered a different country,' Zereda said, and James nodded his head in agreement. He began rummaging around inside a suitcase.

'They say they are starting some big projects in the South. We heard they're going to dig a canal to drain the Sudd, can you imagine? If they did manage to do that it would be a great achievement. There would be movement all year long. But I think it's just a rumour.'

'Could they really drain the whole Sudd?' Nyamakeem asked doubtfully as she put the kisra on the tray next the salad. She was about to transfer the spinach and beef dish to a plate when James stepped out into the alley and handed her a small pouch.

'Such a grand dish from such a generous sister deserves the secret ingredient!'

Curious, Nyamakeem took the pouch and opened it, then squealed in delight.

'Kombo salt!'

Nyamakeem could not remember the last time she had enjoyed a meal so much. With the unique distilled salt – so out of place in Khartoum – the Kombo dish was elevated to another level, and she ate happily as she listened to her new friends describing their aspirations for their new life in the North.

James had graduated from the Juba High School for Boys where he had trained to be a clerk and was planning on finding work in one of the government offices in Khartoum. Nyamakeem could answer none of his questions about this matter: she had not had any dealings with government offices before and didn't even know where they were. Those things were taken care of by Hassan. Zereda had no education; she had successfully evaded recruitment into the local village school as most of the girls in her area had. They had brought all their savings with them, and news of the South.

Sadly, like all the others, the village they came from was far from Nyamakeem's and they brought no news of her family or settlement. They did know that the mission in Doleib Hill was thriving, but otherwise knew nothing of the Shilluk settlements along the White Nile beyond where the steamers moored. Also, their news from the South was disheartening. There was increasing discontent among the people. Development was still poor and Northerners and Egyptians were still being given senior positions in all levels of government. Nyamakeem listened as she ate.

From the sound of it, there was a storm brewing in the South.

Sixteen

Kheir Alseed was eight years old when they saw Hassan for the last time. He kissed them both, counted out the money that he left on the top shelf of her wardrobe and walked away. He did not specify how long he would be gone or why he was going. It had now become a regular occurrence; he was away at the village more than half the year. Nyamakeem and Kheir Alseed had gotten used to managing their days on their own, but they both still felt Hassan's absence in their own way.

The experience of living in Khartoum as an almost-single mother had steeled Nyamakeem. She felt as if she had grown an extra set of eyes. Any trace of her previous naivety had dissipated. There was none of the relaxing atmosphere of her home; everyone was on the move. They were always in a hurry to get somewhere, always ready to move stragglers out of their way. However, with James and Zereda living a bearable distance away she finally had someone to talk to. Their baby daughter was now almost two years old and Nyamakeem adored her, and nicknamed her Zahra, the Arabic name for flower.

Kheir Alseed had little trouble with the language at school. Despite Nyamakeem defaulting to speaking with him in Shilluk at home in Hassan's absence, he had spent several months at the Quaranic school and, alongside memorising Quran, the proper Arabic language had been beaten into him. Nyamakeem watched with admiration as he switched between Arabic and Shilluk with increasing ease, with little from each language affecting the accent of the other. The school was a long distance from their house so they left very early and returned in the late afternoon, but Kheir Alseed still had time to play on the street with the boys in their neighbourhood. Nyamakeem encouraged this as much as she could without affecting his studies; she wanted Kheir Alseed to fit in, to make friends, to feel the sense of belonging that she lacked in Khartoum. But it seemed that he did not entirely belong.

'Mey,' Kheir Alseed had asked her one afternoon, almost four months into his first school year as they walked home from the bus stop after school. 'What am I?'

'What do you mean what are you? You're a boy, of course.'

He kicked small stones as he walked along, stirring up dust. She had told him to stop because it was ruining his sandals.

'What kind of boy?'

Nyamakeem knew what he meant but did not reply. She had known this question would arise sooner or later. She saw the children and parents staring at them whenever she dropped Kheir Alseed off and picked him up. And even if they weren't seen together, his appearance would still draw questions. His name was so Northern and his colour so light they contrasted starkly with the slanted eyes and full mouth that he had in inherited from his mother and grandfather. He also had coarse, short hair that looked nothing like Hassan's shiny mane. And the Sudanese were so obsessed with other people's origins, always asking what tribe they were from, who their family was. Always trying to categorise.

'You're a Sudanese boy, and that's all you need to say.'

Kheir Alseed had appeared to think this over as they walked hand in hand down the narrow street to their house. Other than these questions and the curious looks they attracted, they generally experienced little bothering behaviour in the North. The South Sudanese population that had inhabited some of the El Diyoum neighbourhoods had expanded markedly, and were now a familiar sight around the town. Kheir Alseed played with the boys on their street, and Nyamakeem greeted her neighbours when they passed by each other. When there was an occasion at someone's house, she was invited over or they sent her a plate of food. But she generally kept to herself, lest there be questions about Hassan that she failed to answer correctly. Also, not all her neighbours thought she was their equal. Once, one of the women had knocked on her door and asked her to come and wash some clothes for her. Nyamakeem had been shocked and angrily refused, shutting the door in the confused woman's face.

But with time, Kheir Alseed's tribulations seemed only to grow. Hassan had been gone for five months when Nyamakeem saw Kheir Alseed walked towards her with a torn shirt and his head down. She stopped him at the school gate where she was waiting but he pushed roughly past her, so that she had to hurry behind him to find out what had happened. It was the second time that month.

'Kheir Alseed! You stop this instant and tell me what happened!'

He ignored her and marched on but she caught up and

grabbed his elbow and turned him around to face her. Not only were his clothes torn but he had a dark bruise under his left eye as well.

'You tell me right now or I'm turning around and going to Sit Salma.'

'You'll do no such thing!'

'Then what happened?'

He pulled his elbow from her grasp and turned away but did not walk off. She tried to get him to look at her but he kept turning his face. It looked as if he was fighting back tears.

'He called me wad alkhadim.'

Nyamakeem recoiled in shock. The slave's son? That's what they were calling him?

'Who called you that?'

Kheir Alseed wouldn't tell her, and it wouldn't have made a difference to her anyway because she didn't know the names of his classmates. She had to tell the headmistress about this nonsense and make it stop immediately.

'No!' Kheir Alseed had shouted. 'You'll just make it worse!'

'I can't let them call you that! And you can't keep getting into fights either. You'll get thrown out!'

'I don't care what they call me. It doesn't matter.'

He turned and walked ahead of her, and she followed behind at a distance but not too far for her to hear his complaint.

'If Aboy was here they wouldn't dare this.'

Nyamakeem felt a thick knot in her throat. It didn't bother him that he was being bullied; it bothered him that his father wasn't there to protect him. So early in life and her son had already recognised her weakness. She stood next to him as they waited for their bus, but she did not argue. Because she knew he was right.

One day there was a knock on the door. It was late afternoon and they had just finished their lunch. Nyamakeem wondered who would be calling at this time. She opened the door halfway and peered out at the visitor.

It was a young man – a Northerner – and he stared back at her curiously.

'Are you Hassan's wife?'

Nyamakeem stepped back in surprise. This was the first time anyone had asked her if she was associated with Hassan in any way. She hesitated, wondering if this man was from Hassan's village, snooping around to discover their secret. Or worse; if he was someone Hassan's family had sent to harm her and her son.

'Who are you? How do you know where I live?'

The man appeared to take her questions as a confirmation and reached into his pocket.

'I'm Ibrahim, I manage Hassan's stall at the market. He sent you this.'

He handed her an envelope, still staring at her. She didn't take it. A sound behind her made her turn around as Kheir Alseed came out into the small yard. The man looked at him over her shoulder and she pulled the door closer to.

'Sent me this from where?'

'From the village. He sent it with one of the lorries that arrived this morning.'

It had been almost eight months since Hassan had left; the longest absence yet. Nyamakeem reached out and took the envelope and shut the door in the curious man's face.

'Who was that?' Kheir Alseed asked.

'No one,' she said, crumpling the envelope and hiding it in the folds of her tob. 'He had the wrong house.'

She ordered him into the bathroom to bathe and change. When she heard the splashing water she closed the door to their room and opened the envelope. There was a note inside and some money – a large amount.

'*Āmaarø, I will stay here longer than I anticipated. My mother is not well. I have sent enough money for the next four months and Ibrahim will bring you anything you need. Please send me your news with him. I miss you both.*'

Nyamakeem stared at the note and the money, then sat down heavily on the bed, crumpling the note in her hand. How could he be so comfortable going almost a year without seeing them? Was this it? Had he finally made his choice about which family he would keep and which one he would let go? She heard the bathroom door open and shut and Kheir Alseed's wet flipflops sloshing down the alley. She quickly put the note and money back into their envelope, opened her cupboard and stuffed it behind her clothes on the top shelf. She shut the wardrobe door and leaned her back against it with a sigh, as the words of a man came to her from a distant memory.

৫৩

It had been raining for five straight days; a heavy rain like a monsoon, and the crops were almost ruined. The thick mud sucked at their feet and threatened to swallow the chickens whole. There had been no school for the past week as the children could not leave their pac and the thatched roof of the classroom was about to collapse. The villagers were annoyed but not worried; the ground would suck up the moisture soon.

Nyamakeem sat on the ground at the door to their hut, looking out. From that vantage point she could see the settlement through the opening in their gol's fence. People moved around, inspecting the damage, asking about each other's losses if any, offering to help with what they could. Most of the men had gone out to hunt as they had not been able to for the past few days because of the weather, but a few remained, and she was waiting for one in particular. And then, he came strolling into the gol.

'Näyø!' she called, hurrying out of the hut to greet him at the entrance.

'Teacher Nyamakeem, our prestigious scholar!' her uncle greeted her. 'Our multilingual prodigy! Our ambassador to the Queen of the occupiers!'

Nyamakeem laughed and linked her arm in his, steering him around and back out again.

'Oh,' he whispered conspiringly, 'our mistress of wisdom has a secret! I wonder what it may be!'

Nyamakeem laughed again as they walked arm in arm away from the houses towards the tree line, their bare feet squelching in the mud. In the branches above them the piapac birds called out to each other in their high-pitched 'cheeet' calls, and when they took off in flight the water drops rained down on Nyamakeem and her uncle as they settled down at the foot of a tree.

'So! Who is it? A secret like this must be a suitor.'

Nyamakeem giggled into her hands, feeling both excited and terribly nervous. He was her mother's oldest brother and she loved him dearly. He was also an extremely important person in the Shilluk culture when it came to girls' marriages: the maternal uncle was the first recipient of the bride's bride wealth, and so had an important say in the matter.

'First, dear Uncle, promise me that you will keep this to yourself until things are ready.'

'Of course! Kom gen matho, ka kum de awow. Manage your affairs in silence.' He gave her an exaggerated wink.

Nyamakeem took a deep breath.

'It's a suitor as you guessed,' at which her uncle let out a whooping laugh which he quickly supressed, 'but not your typical suitor.'

'I see,' her uncle said, scrunching his face as if in deep thought. 'He must be of unusual descent. Not even the son of a headsman. The son of the settlement chief? Or maybe even, a nyiirädh, a prince?'

Nyamakeem looked around them to make sure no one was within hearing distance.

'No, none of those. He's a Northerner.'

'What? What did you say? An Arab?'

'A Northerner, dear Uncle. He's a good man and wants to marry me.'

'A Muslim? Nyamakeem! Are you out of your mind? Your father will kill you if he knew you were even talking to this man! Wait,' he stared at her, his eyes growing bigger, 'how do you even know this Northerner? Where did you meet him? At Doleib Hill? Is that what you've been doing this whole time? You tell us you're going to train as a teacher but you're going there to meet him?'

'No! Yes – I mean, I have been doing my training! But I met him there at the hospital, and... and he's been coming back to Doleib Hill to see me.'

'Nyimiyä, my child! What have you done?'

'I haven't done anything! We're only talking! I would never do anything behind your back, you know that.'

Her uncle leaned away from her, looking at her sadly.

'I don't know what this Northerner has told you. But you can't trust him. You will never be happy with him. We are too different, Nyamakeem. And in all cases, how will he marry you if he's a Muslim? They only marry their own kind.'

'They can marry Christians too. I'm a Christian now, remember?' Getting baptised was part of the pre-elementary curriculum the missionaries ran. Nyamakeem had even been given a Christian name by which they called her at Doleib Hill: Angela. But she still prayed to the Shilluk's Juok through their divine king Nyikang, her uncle knew this. He sighed deeply and got to his feet. She followed him up and held his hand.

'Dear uncle, I need your support in this. You can talk to my parents for me, they will listen to you.'

'You know I will do no such thing! And neither will you.' He pulled his hand away and turned to face her. 'Forget about this man, Nyamakeem. You are the daughter of a jal dwong pac, you could choose any man you want from this pac or any other, any man from Muomo to Tonga! This man will never know your true worth. His people will never understand what you are, what it means to be from the dyil and your inherent ownership of this land. He can never appreciate how precious you are.'

'But he does, he knows.'

'Trust me when I tell you my child: you will never be happy with this man. He will be your downfall.'

Her uncle turned around and froze. Nyamakeem looked behind him and saw her father standing a short distance away, leaning on his spear and staring at them.

‧

It had been almost two years since Hassan had left, and five months since the last letter and envelope of money had arrived. Their finances were diminishing rapidly and their rent had gone up for the third time; with the city growing and the influx of Sudanese from all over the country, housing value was skyrocketing. Nyamakeem started reigning in their expenses and cutting down on food. She waited for some word from Ibrahim, but days and weeks passed by with nothing.

She was not the only one who was not faring well. Zereda and James had moved twice, going further and further away seeking cheaper rent. James had been unsuccessful in finding clerical work anywhere, which was not surprising. Nyamakeem was increasingly meeting Southerners who were unable to find work in the fields they had been trained for in the South. There was a vast difference in what they were taught and what was required for the work in the North, and there seemed to be an endless supply of Northerners who could fill the job and were given preference. As a result, James along with countless others found themselves making use of the other skills they had been trained in during their school years: bricklaying, carpentry and manual labour. And with no training of any sort of her own, Zereda worked as a housemaid.

One afternoon, after dropping off Kheir Alseed at school, Nyamakeem headed to the bus stop. Over an hour later she disembarked at the market where she knew Hassan's vegetable stall was. She waited until there was no one nearby before tapping on the open window. Ibrahim's eyes opened wide when he saw her and he quickly stepped out of the door in the back and walked a distance away, beckoning at her to follow. His charade of secrecy irritated her.

'What are you doing here? You know that –'

'That's no business of yours! Where is Hassan?'

Ibrahim looked left and right, rubbing his head.

'I don't know. I haven't heard from him in two months.'

'What do you mean? How is he managing this stall?'

'He isn't. I collect the money at the end of the month and give it to Omar at the shop, and he sends it to Abda Wahab in the village.'

Nyamakeem's blood ran cold when she heard that name: Hassan's hateful, hateful brother. Why was he collecting on Hassan's behalf? Had he finally managed to convince Hassan to stop sending Nyamakeem money?

'I ... I don't know anything else.' Ibrahim stammered, uncomfortable under Nyamakeem's scowl. She glared at him and left.

Sitting on the bus home, she opened her purse and counted the money in it, calculating what remained in addition to the few notes still in the envelope at home. There was barely enough for next month's rent, they needed coal for cooking and she had Kheir Alseed's school fees to pay. She looked out of the window unseeingly, mentally crossing out items from her shopping list that they would have to go without. Every month the list became shorter. Maybe she should have sent Hassan another letter with Ibrahim. But he hadn't responded to the last two letters she had sent, and that angered her even more.

Nyamakeem got off at her stop and stood by the side of the road in the cloud of dust the vehicle left in its wake, in deep, worried thought. She didn't know what was keeping Hassan away from them, or if it was at his will or against it. Maybe he was sick, or maybe his mother was. It was concerning, but the issue of money was the most pressing one. There was no one she could borrow from; the only people she knew were James and Zereda, and she could never ask them; they were even worse off than she was.

Nyamakeem walked down the narrow street towards her house, but instead of going straight she turned right down a small alley. She stopped three houses down and stood in front of a green door, and knocked. Footsteps came to the door, the sound of sandals scraping against the ground, and it opened. The woman looked at Nyamakeem and Nyamakeem looked back.

'Are you looking for help with your washing?'

Seventeen

'Maybe he's sick,' Zereda said to Nyamakeem as they sat in her and James' small room, cutting beans. Zahra played with a set of cloth dolls at her feet and their baby son, Phillip slept on the bed behind Zereda. The room was sparsely furnished and Zereda had lost weight. Nyamakeem could relate to that.

'Maybe,' she said, 'but he could have still sent word. Unless he was too sick to even move his hand.'

'Maybe he is. Maybe he has malaria, you know how serious that can be. It can kill people.'

'The malaria they get up here doesn't come close to what we have back home. Besides,' Nyamakeem sighed, scraping up the leaves from the sides of the tray, 'all those years in the Upper Nile are sure to have given him lifelong immunity.'

The noises from the neighbourhood outside filtered in through the open door. Donkeys neighing, children laughing and screams from an apparent fight somewhere nearby. Zereda looked up at Nyamakeem, and Nyamakeem felt ashamed. James and Zereda had had to move to one of the poorest and most unsafe neighbourhoods in Khartoum and were still struggling to pay rent, while Nyamakeem still lived in the middle-class El Sajana neighbourhood and Kheir

Alseed was in the one of the best schools in the area. She was choosing whose clothes to wash and still considering if she should take on extra work, while Zereda and James had no such choice; they were scrambling to get any work they could. But Nyamakeem could already see the end to this relatively comfortable life.

When she returned home, a notice from their landlord was waiting for her. Nyamakeem had stopped paying rent two months ago; the money she earned from washing and ironing was just enough to feed them and pay for Kheir Alseed's transport to and from school. Counting out the few remaining coins for the hundredth time that week, she decided. She would go to the village and find Hassan.

Nyamakeem had not forgotten her encounter with Hassan's family, especially Abda Wahab and the way he had looked at her that night, how he had referred to her as 'what' and not 'who', a slave not worth their time. But as she lay awake listening to Kheir Alseed's slow breathing, she thought about how Hassan had reassured her that his affairs were all in order 'should anything happen to him.' How happy he was that he had made amends with his family, which meant that their rejection of his wife and son may have thawed, even if just a little bit.

'I'll be gone for no more than a week,' she told Kheir Alseed as she packed. 'I am going to see some relatives in Kosti who have come from my village.'

Nyamakeem didn't want to give Kheir Alseed any ideas about where she was going or if she might find Hassan – or not. He had stopped asking about his father several months ago, but she knew he was waiting for his return.

'I don't understand why I can't go with you.'

Because I have no idea what I'm getting myself into, Nyamakeem thought to herself. She was torn between leaving her son behind, which she had never done before, or taking him along with her and risk exposing him to humiliation or rejection. When she was confident that his father's family would accept him and treat him well, she would take him to them.

'Because you have school. Now you listen to me,' she turned to him and held his face in her hands, masking her worry and biting back tears. 'You listen to what James and Zereda tell you. Don't cause any trouble, don't ask for any more food than what they serve you. You go straight to their house from school – no hanging out on the street.'

Kheir Alseed was not a small boy anymore; he was ten years old and almost as tall as Nyamakeem – he had inherited the impressive Shilluk height. He did not need her to take him to school and back and was capable of moving around the city by bus and tram on his own. While she didn't like to send him and worried constantly until his return, Kheir Alseed sometimes ran errands for Nyamakeem. He did their weekly shopping in the El Sajana market and from even farther away in El Diyoum, when they needed a better price for coal. But it was just the two of them in the world, and with the decision not to take him with her Nyamakeem felt as if she was leaving half her soul behind. She could see that he was about to cry himself and patted his cheek lightly, turning back around to hide her own tears. She counted out some money for him and put it on the top shelf. Then she counted out some more money, which she gave to James and Zereda. That left just enough for the ticket on the Karima train tomorrow morning. Hassan's village was a further half a day's journey by donkey from the station. As the passenger train only went once a week, she would try and find a place back to Khartoum on a cargo train once her business in the village was finished, like they had done all those years ago.

At dawn, Nyamakeem sat on wooden bench in the packed, noisy third-class cabin. She tried to look out the window to the platform where Kheir Alseed and James were standing. She had failed to control her tears that morning when she locked the door to the house, and James had attempted to comfort her and Kheir Alseed as they held each other and cried on the platform. She didn't want to set off another episode now and anyway there were too many people blocking the windows, shouting their good byes to their families and hauling in luggage and children, and buying last minute items from the vendors shouting their merchandise and prices. She also didn't want to lose her spot: she could already see people shifting their bottoms and placing bags and small children in the places vacated by other passengers who had gotten up for a walk.

Nyamakeem tried to calm herself, taking deep breaths and focusing on the image of Hassan in her head and the joy of being with him again after such a long separation. But she wondered for the hundredth time if this was the right thing to do, if her trip would accomplish anything or if it would be a repetition of her first disastrous experience. She worried about what her arrival might mean for Hassan and if their secret would finally be exposed. Would he be happy to see her after all this time? Or would he wish she had never come? She still had time to change her mind and get off the train. But then what?

Always living up to its punctual reputation, the Karima train screeched to a slow move amidst a cacophony of whistling, shouting, laughter and crying, and manoeuvred its way out of the station, swaying side by side, some people still hanging out the windows while a few scuffles broke out in the train where people vied for their own space. Nyamakeem moved her feet out of the way as a woman laid out an empty sack on the ground between their opposing benches and lay her children down, chatting and laughing with the people in the bench beside them. She was squashed on both sides by passengers who clearly did not have tickets to this seat which was meant for three but was now seating five. Amid the loud, happy chaos, Nyamakeem felt loneliness closing in on her, and her alone.

The next evening, she stood on the sand dunes looking down at the village, holding the reigns of the donkey the kind porter had lent her. Nyamakeem had found him standing in the same place at the station when she stepped off the train that afternoon as she and Hassan had done almost a decade before. He had refused to take payment, pointing her instead in the right direction to the village. The sun had set and darkness was gathering quickly around her, and she felt her confidence plummeting further with each passing minute. She was also getting scared; the mountain's shadows cast by the full moon looked as if they were moving. Down in the village there was no light at all. She tried to decide if she should head straight to the house and ask for Hassan. At least that way if there was another confrontation it wouldn't be witnessed. But she wasn't even sure how to find the house on her own; Hassan had led the way last time in the dark, and it had been so long since that first and only visit.

The donkey pulled gently at the reigns. As if in response to the animal's impatience, Nyamakeem heard her stomach growl, and remembered that the last time she had eaten had been a modest breakfast on the train the day before. She had been too anxious to eat anything since then and had politely declined several friendly invitations from her fellow passengers to join their meals. Perhaps she should at least have something to eat before venturing down into the village; she would most likely need all her energy for whatever awaited her. The donkey pulled the reigns again, this time moving away from her and heading towards the mountains, as if it knew where to go. Nyamakeem followed, and a few minutes later was in the small yard of the shack. Well that was decided, she thought, and sat down.

The next morning, Nyamakeem arose with a heavy head: she had barely slept all night from the dread of what was to come, and from the fear of being so alone in the darkness. Her short dozes on the hard ground had been interrupted by the repeated feeling of something touching her feet and face, startling her back awake. When the moon momentarily disappeared behind a cloud and the darkness around her and inside her suddenly became absolute, she had gotten on her knees and prayed to both Jesus and Juok, calling out to Nyikang and every ancestor she could remember. In the bright sunlight of morning, looking at the donkey standing obediently by the wall, she felt as if she had been in this shack for weeks. She got up stiffly and collected her belongings. There was nothing for breakfast and she had no appetite anyway.

She decided to leave the donkey where it was and would come for it later; either to bring it back to the village or to ride it back to Karima. She opened the door and cried out in terror at the tall figure standing silently outside.

The young nomad leaned on a large rock and stared at her curiously. His dirty clothes were too big for him and torn in several places. His cap was perched at an angle on his head, and he was chewing a worn miswak branch with leisure. A few goats were grazing behind him on nothing. They were perched on the stones and high up on the rocks, jumping expertly from height to height. Nyamakeem stared back at the young man, breathing heavily and anxiously wondering what she would do if he attacked her. She had nothing to defend herself with and no one to call out to for help. She realised vaguely that this was the same situation she would be in when she met her in-laws if Hassan wasn't there: no way to defend herself, no one to ask for help. The young nomad looked at her with interest for a few more seconds, then pushed lazily off the rock and called to his goats with a click of the tongue, and turned away without giving her a second glance. Nyamakeem let her breath out. She waited until she could see him walking across the sand dunes before pulling the door shut behind her and heading out towards the village.

Nyamakeem walked between the scattered houses, unsure where to go. She remembered they had walked down a straight road then turned left, dipping a little then levelling out. The black gates had been visible at the end of the street. It was very early in the morning but the streets were full of people, mainly men and boys. They were carrying hoes and axes and heading away from the direction of the dunes, towards their fields Nyamakeem assumed. A couple of donkey carts driven by two young boys crossed in the opposite direction with some sacks and steel boxes on their decks. A man on a donkey balancing two large steel pails on either side knocked loudly on a door that Nyamakeem passed. It was immediately answered by a little girl carrying a small pot into which the man measured some milk.

The activity both lifted her spirits and worried her: the lively atmosphere and bright sunshine displaced that earlier gloomy image she had held of the village and breathed hope into her endeavour. But she worried that if the encounter was as terrible as last time, it would be in front of all these people which would not only embarrass her greatly but would also expose Hassan. She kept her face covered with her tob and looked down as she walked slowly through the streets, but she knew that with her height and visibly darker skin she was hardly blending in.

Nyamakeem turned left and followed the incline of the road which she thought she remembered from last time. She walked close to the wall but still felt exposed, and just as she was wondering if she had taken the wrong road she saw the high black gates in front of her. They looked even more intimidating than she remembered. She approached them slowly and hesitantly lifted her hand to knock. It was shaking. She looked around her and waited until the street was completely deserted. Then she knocked on the gates.

Immediately, she heard footsteps hurrying towards her and the gate was flung open. A young boy stood at the door looking at her curiously. She stared at him. He looked two or three years younger than Kheir Alseed.

'Who are you?' he asked, his heavy northern accent making the words sound funny. Nyamakeem took in the nose and the wide forehead.

'I'm ... I'm ...' she stammered, unable to look away from his face, unable to recollect any of the lines she had prepared. She stopped, took a deep breath and started again.

'I'm Nyamakeem. Who are you?'

'Hamid,' he answered confidently. 'Hamid Hassan Kheir Alseed.'

It was as if she had been slapped. She heard the name, but she also saw the face: it was like looking at a small version of Hassan. He even sounded a little bit like him. Only this boy looked so much more like Hassan than Kheir Alseed ever had. Hassan had a son – another son.

But of course, she thought, as she stared at the boy in front of her. She wasn't that surprised. Of course, his family would make him remarry. No wonder he had been spending so much time here.

The boy looked at her and shifted on his feet, itching to get this boring meeting over with. He kept his hand on the door, leaning out and looking this way and that. Nyamakeem cleared her throat.

'Where ... where is your father?'

The boy stopped moving and stared at her.

'And what business is it of yours?'

A woman emerged from behind the door and moved the boy out of the way. She was tall – almost as tall as Nyamakeem – and handsome with thick, deep shulookh grooves running in three vertical lines down her cheeks, her shiny black hair parted in the middle and wrapped in braids around her ears. She was dressed in a white tob. The lack of henna on her hands and feet contradicted with her overall image of self-care. She looked Nyamakeem up and down with a sneer. Nyamakeem looked back, trying to look confident. She was no common beggar or fraud. She had a genuine cause. She cleared her throat.

'My name is Nyamakeem. Hassan is my –'

'I know who you are,' the woman hissed menacingly, taking a step forward and pulling the door to a narrow opening. 'I knew you would show up sooner or later. What did you think you would find here? Did you think you could just prance into this house and lay your filthy, heathen hands on whatever property you liked? You and your walad alharam?'

'What? No, no I just wanted –'

'What you *want* is irrelevant. There is nothing for you here. Hassan had only one lawful wife, and you are looking at her. Allagiya bit Mohamed!'

Nyamakeem stepped back fearfully, overwhelmed by the woman's hostility. Allagiya took another threatening step towards her.

'He had one wife and one son. You are not entitled to a single date seed. Not one gold coin.'

Nyamakeem felt her throat constrict, was unable to swallow.

'What … what do you mean "he had"?'

The woman sneered at her. 'Hassan is dead. He has been for over a year. No one told you? Now you know, you can leave!' and she slammed the gate closed, bolting it from the inside.

Eighteen

Nyamakeem and Kheir Alseed moved out of the one-bedroom and were once again holed up in half a house. They moved as close to the school as was possible to cut down on transport fees, but it was a much poorer part of town with disorganised housing and narrow streets. Nyamakeem sold her metal beds, the armchairs, the few tools Hassan had left behind, and soon started selling her gold and beaded jewellery. Once they had settled in she started knocking on the doors of the bigger houses farther down the road looking for housework and washing. She refused to let Kheir Alseed work in the market during or after school; his studies were his one and only priority, she told him. They would manage on her meagre earnings one way or another.

'And what happens after I finish school? What then?'

'Then the University. Or an apprenticeship,' she said resolutely. 'And a proper job.'

Nyamakeem worried at the growing note of resentment in Kheir Alseed's voice every time they discussed their financial situation. He had taken the forced move badly and his sullenness increased with each item she sold. He hated that she was working in other people's houses, and his fighting at school became more frequent. Nyamakeem worried his schoolwork would suffer and tried everything she could to maintain some kind of normalcy around the house. She made sure his school clothes were always clean, she stitched the holes and frayed ends quickly before they turned grey and expanded. She looked with sadness as his feet outgrew his tired sandals and calculated how much a new pair would cost and how many more loads of washing she would have to do in order to afford them. She would have to find extra work.

One morning she waited until Kheir Alseed had left for school, then emerged from the house with a small, covered pot in one hand, wooden crate-turned-table in the other, a couple of shallow steel dishes, and a bag of bread under her arm. The market was almost half an hour walk from the house and had a section dedicated to women merchants who sold all sorts of items: talih wood for smoking the skin, karkar, melted and perfumed animal fat for hair, and weaved baskets and mats. There was also a section for selling food. She entered from the end of the line of sellers and found an empty spot where she put her things down. But before she could arrange her things on the box a woman descended on her.

'Hey! What do you think you're doing?'

Nyamakeem stammered in alarm, but the woman gave her no chance.

'You think you could just sit wherever you want? This spot is taken! Move on!'

Nyamakeem hastily picked up her belongings and fled. After two more failed tries, she abandoned the women's section altogether and went deeper into the market, finally finding a spot far removed from the bustling centre but where she could set up her modest food selling service unchallenged. She had decided to start with fava beans, as they were cheapest to produce. She had spent far more than she could afford on a modest measurement of Masalamiya beans – the best and most expensive type – washed and soaked them overnight, cooked them over a low heat for several hours until they were soft, and added salt, dry fennel and sesame oil. Her location was not a busy one, but there was a group of tobacco stands nearby where men collected and chatted as they filled their bags. She put a modest price on each plateful of fava beans and waited.

For the first hour no one bought anything, though a few men asked her what she was selling and for how much. She was thinking she maybe should have fought for a space in the women's market when she heard a faint whistle from a distance. In a few minutes the market was flooded with men dressed in everything from smart Safari suits to sweaty coveralls, talking loudly, lighting cigarettes, washing oil off their hands, and absolutely starving. The lunch hour had commenced. By the end of the second hour Nyamakeem was sold out.

Nyamakeem divided her week between her different jobs and worked hard in each one. In addition to the fava beans she sold boiled eggs, falafels and aubergine salad. The other women in the market sold steaming plates of mullah and asida, fried meats, stews and sweet desserts, but she had neither the skill to cook these meals that were not native to her, nor the money to be able to afford their ingredients. She did, however, add millet porridge and Kombo twice a week which attracted some fellow Southerners and a few Northerners who had been in the South and were familiar with it. Soon she had a recurring set of customers and was able to count on a relatively stable income.

Nyamakeem thought about her village almost every day now. She woke up and went to sleep longing to be back in the safety of her father's gol. At night while she lay awake listening to Kheir Alseed talking in his sleep, she imagined she could see the cows' dancing shadows on the wall of their room, prancing around the low light of the kerosene lamp. She wondered how her family was: if her brothers and sisters had married, if her parents were in good health. If they ever thought about her. And if they did think about her, if it was with love or disappointment. She thought about all the decisions she had made and if, now that she knew what she knew, she would have done things differently. She didn't know. She wondered if she did go back to them, if all would be forgiven. She didn't know.

⚮

It had been Nyamakeem's last day of training at Doleib Hill and she was packing her remaining belongings. The room was empty. She looked at Alek's bed with a sigh, wishing her friend was here. It seemed like it was yesterday that she had stepped into this room for the first time, tearful and afraid, clutching the small leather pouch her mother had given her and in which Nyamakeem had placed a fistful of dirt from the ground of their homestead. She looked at the leather pouch now with its contents still inside. It had been a way to carry her home with her wherever she went, and an implicit assurance that she would always find her way back no matter how far she strayed.

'All packed, dear Angela?'

Sister Sarah poked her head into the room. At Doleib

Hill Nyamakeem was called by her Christian name which she sometimes forgot on her long holidays back at the pac.

'Yes, almost. I didn't realise I had so many things.'

'Yes, we do tend to accumulate belongings. But you've also been here for so long. I think you've been here longer than anyone else.'

'Almost six years.'

'That's right. And you've come such a long way. I'm really proud of all the progress you've made. And now you're going back to your people to share your knowledge and help enlighten the younger generations. May the Lord bless you.'

Outside, a small group of fowl strolled around on the grass and scattered dramatically when Nyamakeem walked past them towards the hospital grounds. She took her time walking down the path that she had passed over countless times; first with Alek, and then alone to meet Hassan. The hospital buildings had expanded in the years that she had been there. It was serving a larger population, now that it had gained the people's trust. Nyamakeem stopped to watch a group of nurses walking across the yard from the administrative building towards the wards. She still admired their uniforms and the important work that they did. In another lifetime, perhaps, she could have been one of them.

'Still dreaming of joining the white ranks, Āmaarø?'

Hassan stood at the end of the path, smiling at Nyamakeem. That smile, she thought; the smile that was just for her. The smile that managed to draw her out of any mood no matter how dark. She realised she was still holding the leather pouch that carried her bit of home, and tried to smile back, but instead burst into tears, as the hopelessness of their situation filled the air between them.

They had been standing in the middle of the pac, just a few metres away from their homestead from which Nyamakeem's mother and stepmother had just emerged, wondering what all the shouting was about. Other people had come out of their homesteads as well and stood at a distance, watching curiously. But once they had seen who it was the chief was shouting at, they stepped back in embarrassment. It made no difference though, because Nyamakeem's father was shouting loudly enough for the entire settlement to hear. Nyamakeem had trembled with fear and shame. She wished the earth could split open and swallow her.

'Fraternising with a Northerner! An Arab! When your mothers and grandmothers are slaving away in their households at this minute! Buried in their desecrated grounds with no lyel, away from their families and ancestors? How dare you!'

'But Wä, it's not what you think, he's a good ma–'

'Silence!' her father had thundered. Nyamakeem shrunk down to the ground, whimpering miserably. 'I sent you to learn the language of these colonisers so that you would protect your people from them, and what do you do? You spend your days running around with a jalabi who would throw a noose around your neck the minute you turn around!'

Nyamakeem hung her head and wept.

'Omiye,' she had heard her uncle clear his throat and say in a low voice. 'Brother, it was just a wild thought. Nyamakeem has no intention of going forward with anything. I assure you.'

'I have never been more disappointed in anyone before in my life. I put my trust in you and you betrayed me. You are banned from leaving this pac! And,' her father advanced on her and leaned down threateningly, 'and if I ever hear you have spoken with this man again you will be no daughter of mine!'

Hassan looked down at his hands as Nyamakeem wiped her tears. They sat side by side, leaning against the trunk of a palm tree, their back to the Mission. The late afternoon sun cast them in a large, spiky shade that shrouded their figures like a blanket. Nyamakeem had prepared herself for this moment; had been preparing herself since the night she had cried herself to sleep after her father had threatened to disown her. If her uncle hadn't appealed to let her at least get her things back from the school, and that he would personally accompany her and bring her back, she wouldn't even be here.

'Let me speak to him, Āmaarø. I've been asking you for months to let me meet your family.'

'Hassan, my father will throw a spear through your eye before you even step foot in the pac. I've never in my life seen him so angry.'

'Nyamakeem, this nonsense about slavery is ancient, you know that. There are dozens, hundreds of Northerners who are married to Southerners and who are living happily and peacefully with their families. We're not the first.'

'I do not know about these other people. It's hopeless, Hassan. My father is not the man to change his mind so simply, especially in something like this.' Nyamakeem stood up heavily. 'I'm not able to go against him.'

'Then come away with me! Right now. We can get married and go to the North, or we could go to Bahr

Alghazal or Wau. You could teach there, or you could train to be a nurse. We could even look for your friend, Alek.'

'Are you out of your mind? I could never do such a thing!'

'Āmaarø, I won't leave you. Either I come with you to the pac or you come away with me. Please,' he held both her hands in his. 'Please, Nyamakeem. I want you to be my nyaara, the mother of my children. You and no one else.'

Nyamakeem's uncle knocked on the dormitory door once, then several times, bringing Sister Sarah out in a piously irritated huff.

'Yes?'

'Where is Nyamakeem?'

'Who? Who is that?'

'What do you mean who is that, woman? Nyamakeem! The teacher! She came to get her clothes.'

'You mean Angela,' Sister Sarah said with disapproval. 'Her name is Angela. She just came in a minute ago, I'll get her.'

She stepped back inside and shut the door in Nyamakeem's uncle's face. He stepped out of the roof's shade and into the sunlight, his hands behind his back, looking around at the mission and its inhabitants. He heard the door open behind him and turned around.

Sister Sarah was back, but she was alone, and looked confused.

'Her things are all gone, but she's not in the room. I saw her come in myself.'

'What do you mean? Where is she?'

'I, I don't know where she is.'
Nyamakeem was gone.

⌘

Nyamakeem's work in the market was important not just as a source of income, but also as a source of news. She listened intently as her customers read the newspapers out loud and argued about the dying days of British occupation, about the countries around them that had gained their independence, and how it was their turn now that the British had granted the Sudanese the right for self-determination two years before. She came to recognise the names of Ismail Alazhari, Abdulrahman Almahdi, Almirghani. Politicians who were tribal leaders, tribal leaders who were politicians. Just like the men in the market, some of these leaders were for independence while others wanted the British to stay. Next year, in 1956, they would decide. All this interested her only a little, though. What interested her was the bits of information from the South.

'A mutiny in the South!'

Nyamakeem paused with a spoon full of aubergine salad in mid-air. The market had been particularly quiet that afternoon and there were no Southerners around at all. The two men sitting on the low stools in front of her were sharing a newspaper, concentrating on the lower half of a page. One of them held onto his fava bean sandwich with the other hand and brought it up to his mouth for a bite. The other seemed to have forgotten his.

'Three hundred killed! Three hundred! Those criminals!'

Nyamakeem's listened with mounting horror as the

men read out the news of a rebellion in the South in which soldiers from the Equatorian Corps had killed over three hundred Northerners the previous week – soldiers and civilians. It had happened in Torit and had been followed by mutinies in other garrisons. She looked up from the sandwich she was making into the eyes of the two men who were looking straight at her and held her breath. Just a minute ago they had been happily swallowing her sandwiches. Now they stared at her with suspicion, as if it was her they were reading about in the paper. Nyamakeem looked back down and busied herself with the food and cleaning up the crumbs until the two men got up and left. They didn't pay for their sandwiches. She quickly gathered her things and hurried home.

It seemed that the men's sentiment was shared by everyone as news of the killings spread, and people recognised family members and friends, entire families who had perished in the uprisal. Nyamakeem was now facing looks of hatred and dirty comments as she walked down the street to and from work. Two of the families she regularly cleaned for told her they no longer required her services. Her food selling business suffered as even her regular customers angrily boycotted her. Even the Southerners, sensitive to the hostility in the air, stopped coming and their presence in the market decreased markedly. The news would die down eventually, but the undercurrent of unrest in the South constantly simmered beneath the conversations Nyamakeem heard. It felt as if the storm that had been brewing for the past several years had finally arrived.

Nyamakeem kept her head down and cut her five days

at the market down to only two, trying to make up for it by finding work in houses farther away. She stretched their food rations even more. She and Kheir Alseed ate one meal a day. Kheir Alseed had red tea and dried bread – if there was any – in the morning, and would not eat again until he came back from school. He was almost thirteen years old now. Looking at him reminded Nyamakeem of both Hassan and her own father, and the constant reminders pushed her into-ever deepening sadness.

Five months after the mutiny in the South, the Sudanese voted for independence from colonial rule, and the British marched back to their shrinking kingdom. People took to the streets celebrating the birth of their country in huge processions, singing national songs, waving flags and ululating. Nyamakeem and Kheir Alseed walked on the side lines of a procession passing down the road near the train station, revelling in the uplifting scene. Despite their personal circumstances it was impossible not to join the celebration of independence from the foreign invaders who had been governing their lives for decades.

But for Nyamakeem, the celebration was marred by the ongoing news of hostilities in the South from which news of armed movements attacking convoys and patrols continued to arrive. The danger seemed to be localised to specific areas and directed towards armed government posts, not civilians, but she still worried constantly about her family. She wondered if it was time for her and Kheir Alseed to go home.

It was the evening of Kheir Alseed's sixteenth birthday and Nyamakeem had made his favourite okra stew with a few bits of good meat that she had saved for all week. She took only small bites and left most of the dish for him. There wasn't enough to satiate both of them; there rarely was. It was November, and the weather was beginning to cool. Soon she would have to search for talih wood for the coal burner that would warm their small room. Kheir Alseed would also need a new shawl to wear outside in the biting winter wind. His current shawl had fraying edges and several holes. Nyamakeem wouldn't need to buy one, though; she had kept all of Hassan's clothes and shoes. She was saving his shawl for Kheir Alseed, for when he finished school and applied at the Gordon Memorial College, which was now a university. He had outgrown all of Hassan's jallabiyas long before.

Kheir Alseed chewed his food silently, looking down at the bones he was collecting at the edge of the tray.

'I want to see my father's grave.'

Nyamakeem. almost choked on her food and suppressed a fit of coughing with difficulty.

'What did you say?'

He didn't look up at her and continued to eat slowly. She regained herself and cleared her throat, then fell silent, thinking furiously.

'Why? Why do you want to see it? Why now?'

'Why not?' he looked up and she saw the sharp light in his eyes. It looked as if he had been thinking about this for some time and was prepared for a fight. Nyamakeem glared back at him until he lowered his gaze. She had been caught off guard, but was not surprised. She looked down at the tray and took a small bite, thinking about how to navigate the conversation she had always known would come.

'I don't know where his grave is. He drowned in the river and these Northerners bury their drowned bodies wherever they find them. Not in a graveyard.'

'Well then, I'll go and look for it myself. I'll ask my uncles.'

She looked up at him in alarm.

'What? What are you talking about? How do you even know if you have any uncles?'

'It's not like my father fell out of a tree. Everyone has family. I'm going to find his family – *my* family – and visit his grave. And then,' he looked down and shuffled the bones around nervously, 'then I'll ask about my inheritance.'

'You'll do no such thing!' Nyamakeem stood up and glowered down at him, breathing heavily. But then he stood up as well and she found herself looking up at him instead. He had grown taller than her in just one summer. He wasn't a child anymore and was now making his own decisions.

'Why not? Where is my father's family?'

'Your father doesn't have any family! You don't have any uncles! The only family you have is me!'

'I don't believe you! We Sudanese are like rabbits, we have a hundred relatives and more! How can I be the only person in the world who has just his mother? What is it that you aren't telling me!'

They glared at each other. Nyamakeem was struggling internally, fighting with herself between what she desired – to forget forever – and what she knew her son wanted – to belong.

'Tell me who they are. I just want to know. I want to know who my father was. I want to know who I am. I don't remember what his voice sounded like anymore. I barely remember his face!'

Nyamakeem felt all her defences coming crashing down. Kheir Alseed towered over her, but he was suddenly just a little boy, a little boy who just wanted his father. Memories of him still learning to walk, wearing Hassan's big shoes that kept tripping him up, his laughter when Hassan tickled him, his happiness when Hassan brought him pieces of sugar cane and sweet peanut candy. Kheir Alseed hadn't even said a proper goodbye to his father; he had been fast asleep when Hassan had stepped out of the house for the last time. Nyamakeem saw the way Kheir Alseed watched James when he played with Zahra and Phillip, how carefully he followed whenever James was teaching Phillip how to do something. More than once she had sensed that Kheir Alseed's fights with Phillip were more about getting James's attention than anything else. He was constantly longing for a father. And how could Nyamakeem blame him for that?

Even as a grown woman, she constantly longed for her family back in Malakal, always wondering if they would take her back. Twice in the past year alone she had gone as far as put some money aside for the train and steamer fares that would take them to her home and back. Twice she had taken that money back to pay for their expenses. And there rarely passed a week when she didn't think of Hassan, reminded of him by something she had seen or heard, longing for him when things got difficult. Both Nyamakeem and Kheir Alseed fought back tears as Hassan's memory hovered around them in the room. Who was she to deny him what he so desperately wanted to know?

She told him everything. How she had met Hassan, her family's refusal and their elopement, their decision to move North for Kheir Alseed's sake. Their encounter with Hassan's family. Hassan's gradual disappearance from their lives. Her trip to the village, and her encounter with his other family – his 'lawful' family.

Kheir Alseed stared at Nyamakeem in disbelief. It was a mistake, she thought to herself, telling him all this. She sighed.

'Your family – your father's family – was not happy about our marriage and they practically disowned us. Disowned you. That's why we live here, like this.'

She looked up into the shock in his eyes. She tried to find the words to describe the situation that would keep their dignity intact, but also keep any closed doors firmly shut.

'I'm not telling you this so that you can try and talk to them or contact them in any way. I just want you to know that –' But what did she want him to know? That he was an outcast just like her? That he was an outcast *because* of her?

'Why didn't you tell me any of this before? You just said he drowned.'

'He did drown. He must have drowned.'

'Yes, but you didn't say he drowned near his own home, near his own family – his other family – of which I know nothing about. You didn't tell me I have a brother.'

She looked up from her hands at him. The air around them turned suddenly cool as she looked into the dark blankness of his eyes, and found herself looking into those of his father.

'And what about my inheritance?'

She flinched.

'Who put that idea in your head?'

'No one put the idea in my head,' he said angrily. 'I know I have an inheritance, everyone does. And from what you describe, Aboy had a lot of money, and that money is rightfully mine!'

'I know nothing about that. We have nothing from them, we want nothing from them —'

'Yes we do! We want what's ours! I want what's *mine*.'

'We have nothing there ya Kheir Alseed! They will never give you anything! They want nothing to do with you!'

'I don't care what they want! I'm not living the rest of my life like this! How could I dream of going to university when my mother is a housemaid, if I have even a single gold coin that is rightfully mine?'

'What did you say to me?'

He turned his face away from her, embarrassed, but he was not prepared to back down.

'This is no way to live and you know it. How long are you going to slave away in people's houses and put up with their shit? Even if I find work, how long will it take us to live like other people do? How much longer do we have to keep counting every single penny, barely make rent, always be hungry?'

Nyamakeem felt his words cut into her like bits of broken glass. But she could not argue with his logic. And she was so, so tired of it all, of the constant effort of trying to hold their lives together.

'Let's drop this now. We'll talk about it some other time.'

'But mother, I –'

'I said we'll talk about it later!'

Nyamakeem picked up the tray with the abandoned food. It was the first time they had left something uneaten in many years, but just looking at it nauseated her. She felt his eyes boring into her back. Her mind was reeling. She needed time to organise her thoughts.

She heard no snoring that night and knew that he was lying awake, just like her. Her mind was in turmoil: should she let him go and find out for himself what they were like? Perhaps when they saw him and saw how much he looked like his father they might give in. They say time sometimes heals wounds and softens edges. Often with time come regrets, second thoughts and wishes that things had been different. And no matter what, blood was always thicker than water. Surely, the worst that could happen was that they would turn him away with nothing, and then he would know for sure. He might even be able to find Hassan's grave and that would give him some form of closure. Nyamakeem thought about Hassan's son, Hamid. Maybe he and Kheir Alseed could even be friends.

Nyamakeem remembered the day Hassan told her about all the riches they had inherited from their deceased uncle, how he had counted all the assets and even projected how much they would be worth when their son came of age. It had been so much. Her son was positioned on a mountain of gold – but instead he lived with her, the son of a housemaid, a Southerner in the North, with nothing to his name. It was not fair of her to hold him back.

Maybe they would accept him.

When she left for work the next morning Kheir Alseed

was still asleep. She put the tea pot over the low embers of the coal burner for him to drink when he got up for school, watching him where he lay and trying to remember what it had been like when it was the three of them. She couldn't. All day at work her mind turned this way and that. Let him go? Make him stay? She couldn't decide. She went about her duties in a daze and kept mixing up the orders at the market. She barely heard the news the men sitting in front of her were discussing. The brief euphoria that had enveloped the country after independence had died down long ago. There had been problems in the government for weeks; they were fighting over something or another. And the unrest in the South was getting worse.

When Nyamakeem returned later in the evening – later than she usually did – she brought a small bag of bananas to sweeten the air. She and Kheir Alseed would talk about it reasonably. She would explain her concerns to him and try and make him understand that just the thought of him being humiliated or hurt was too much for her to handle. But she would respect his decision, whatever it may be.

Kheir Alseed wasn't home. The tea pot was empty and the embers dumped outside near the door were cold. She cleaned the house, collected the clothes to be washed and lit a few coals on the burner for a small pot of lentils to cook. Evening turned to night and there was still no sign of Kheir Alseed. He was angry, she knew. This wasn't the first time he had stayed out late when he was pouting about something. He was a big boy now – almost a man. If he needed space she would give it to him.

Nyamakeem ate her dinner alone and left most of the

food for him. She was exhausted from staying up the night before and working all day and was asleep the moment her head touch the pillow. She woke up a few hours later and looked over at his bed. It was empty. She got up and walked to the outhouse, calling his name in a low voice. No reply. She came back inside and sat down, her insides starting to churn as the worry grew. He was just taking his time, she thought to herself. He'll be back in the morning.

But he wasn't, and before the sun was fully up in the sky the next day she locked the front door and headed to work, but only briefly. The argument from the day before had been playing nonstop in her head, and she wondered. For the first time in a long time, Nyamakeem crossed the El Sajana market to find Ibrahim, the boy who managed Hassan's first stall.

'Yeah, I saw him,' he said, leaning on the side of his stall.

'What? You saw him? Yesterday?'

'Not yesterday, last week. He came here asking about Hassan.'

'Last *week*? What did you tell him?'

Ibrahim looked over his shoulder then back at Nyamakeem, talking in a low voice.

'He asked me where to find his family – Hassan's family, and I told him.'

Nyamakeem felt a huge pit open up in her stomach and everything drop in. So that was how Kheir Alseed knew about his uncles, maybe even about his inheritance. She couldn't work out how he had even known about Ibrahim, then remembered that Ibrahim was bringing them letters and money at the house until Kheir Alseed was nine years old.

'Why didn't you tell me about this?'

'He's your son. How should I know he was running away from you?'

'He wasn't running away!'

'Well, he's not here now. If he really did go the village like he said was planning to do, he'll probably already be there by now.'

She cursed him in Shilluk up to his fifth ancestor as he turned around and stepped back into his ticket stall, indifferent to her wrath. At dawn the next day she was sitting in the corner of the cargo train heading to Karima, as there was no passenger train that day. She had used the last bit of gold she had – her wedding ring – to pay the fare.

Nineteen

It was only one day and night, but Nyamakeem felt as if she had spent her entire lifetime on the train. She ate nothing, slept none at all, and cried continuously. It felt as if – except for that very first time that she had travelled to the village with Hassan – every journey was doomed to be miserable. When she disembarked at the station the next morning the first thing she saw was the porter standing in his usual place. It had been six years since she had seen him last, but they both recognised each other immediately and greeted one another like old friends. He told her his donkey had died.

The station was strangely empty, and Nyamakeem could hear military music playing from a radio in one of the offices. She didn't know what that meant, and when the man told her that there had been a military coup in Khartoum, she didn't care. The man led Nyamakeem out of the station towards the main road where a large lorry was waiting, already half full of people. She got on and sat down near the window, avoiding the curious looks she was attracting and keeping her face covered. Around her the people were talking about the coup and how General Aboud had seized power. After two long hours the lorry was full and the driver geared it into motion. They moved through the streets then out into the open and headed south.

Nyamakeem stared out the window at the passing villages but did not see a thing.

The lorry broke down less than an hour later. Nyamakeem cursed and cursed, wishing she had just asked the porter for another animal to ride instead of this stupid vehicle. She stayed on the bus while the other passengers walked around and chitchatted. Whatever it was that was broken was taking time to fix. The passengers invited Nyamakeem to join their meals but she refused. She couldn't have eaten if she had wanted to; she felt sick to her stomach.

Finally, the bus started moving. It was already late afternoon. By the time Nyamakeem got off near the village mosque it was already dark. It was as if she had been dropped back into the memory of that first night. She hurried through the silent streets towards the large house at the far east of the village. The village had changed a little: there were more houses, extensions of the old ones where families had expanded. At the hated gates, she stopped to catch her breath. It was dark but she could see a faint light from within. Their father's lamp, of course.

She knocked loudly on the gates. Almost immediately they were thrown open, as if the family were expecting someone. She shrunk back as Abdal Wahab Kheir Alseed stepped out and advanced on her.

'What do you want, slave?'

'My son, where is he!'

'What son? That wad alharam is nowhere around her.'

'He's here! He came here, I know it! Where –'

The blow came out of nowhere. Nyamakeem didn't even realise she had been hit until she found herself in the dirt, her ears ringing. Before she registered what had happened he kicked her in the stomach, knocking all the air out of her. She let out a soundless scream.

'Who do you think you are, coming here and making demands? You think because my brother dragged you out of that jungle that you have some right to claim?'

She tried to get up and he kicked her again.

'If you want to find your son you can search for him at the bottom of the river!'

She rolled over just in time to avoid his foot landing on her face and to hear the gates slam shut behind of her.

The river!

Nyamakeem got up and ran with all her might down the street towards the date gardens that she had seen before, and which Hassan had told her long ago ended at the river Nile. She tripped and fell over half a dozen times, and her tob caught on branches and tore as she made her way through the dark forest towards the water. She did not know if she was going in the right direction until she blundered out of the trees and reached the riverside. It was a moonless night and scattered clouds obscured the stars. She could see nothing, but heard the lapping of the water against the bank below. She looked over the side into a solid wall of darkness.

'Kheir Alseed! My son! Kheir Alseed!'

There was no response. She ran further upstream, looking over the side, then back down again.

'Kheir Alseed! Where are you?! Answer me please!'

Nothing.

She stayed all night by the water. When the sun had fully risen the next day, she had walked the entire length of the village up and down the river several times, weeping hysterically. A few villagers saw her and shivered at the raving black woman with her ripped and dusty clothes roaming all over the waterfront. By mid-afternoon she was about to collapse. She hobbled back through the gardens and headed west towards the mountain, towards the old shack that seemed to exist just to provide her some form of shelter whenever she came to this cursed village. She collapsed on the ground in a weeping mess. Later, she did not hear the knock at the door. When the knock came again, she crawled towards the door and opened it, not caring who or what was asking to come in.

It was the Arab nomad from all those years ago. He looked at her with a blank face, taking in her dirty clothes, the debris in her hair, the anguish in her face. He turned away without a word, but when he returned less than an hour later, it was with a thin blanket, some food and a leather pouch of water.

Nyamakeem stayed for two weeks, searching for any trace of her son, but to no avail. Fearful of what the Kheir Alseeds might do if they saw her around the village, she stayed in the shack during the day and roamed the village streets and the water front at night. She called to Kheir Alseed in a low voice, leaning over the side. Twice she saw a dark shape in the water and lunged for it, but on both occasions, it was nothing: a large piece of driftwood, and the carcass of a dead sheep. She felt she was losing her mind with grief and lost count of the days. She forgot where she was, often mistaking the trees behind her for the palm trees at Doleib Hill; the river in front of her for the White Nile where her brothers used to fish. Twice, she came across figures lurking around in the dark. She asked them:

'Have you seen my son in the water? In the moya?'

In her state of mind, she spoke a mix of Chollo and broken Arabic. They heard 'moya' – moya they understood.

⚬~⚬

On the fifteenth day, as Nyamakeem sat leaning against the wall of the shack, staring at the sky, exhausted from her night search, she heard movement outside the door. She got up slowly to answer the door for the nomads who had been bringing her food and water this whole time, but before she took a step forward it was roughly kicked in and the small yard was suddenly filled with shouting men.

She cried out in terror as they advanced on her, sticks in hand, swearing and hurling racist slurs and threats. She backed against the wall and raised her arm to protect her fact, but it was yanked back down and she found herself face to face with Hassan. It was him, he had come back from the dead. In her terror, she wet herself.

'You are not welcome here woman!' Hamid Hassan Kheir Alseed roared at her, raising his stick high and waving it over her head. 'Leave now or you'll join your bastard son at the bottom of the river.'

'You! You were the one!'

Hamid Kheir Alseed brought the stick down and it crashed into the wall beside her head. She screamed and crouched to the ground, covering her head as splinters of mud and rock rained down on her. She felt him lean down next to her and growl into her ear.

'Yes, me! I was the one to teach him a lesson! Coming here and trying to embarrass us in front of everyone! Claiming he had a right to our wealth! He wasn't so brave in the end when he was crying out for you like a little girl. Get out of here, or Mohamed Altahir will send you to join him!'

Part III

Twenty

Fatima sat motionless, staring at Mohamed Altahir through a gap by the door hinges into the men's deiwan. He avoided Habiba's eyes and stared down at his hands, speechless in front of his wife. Her parents only came here when there was serious business to be discussed, like a marriage proposal or a difficult health decision. Fatima had not felt guilty eavesdropping; her father had been out of sorts all day and had stayed home from both funerals, which was highly unusual.

'You ... why?' Habiba asked her husband.

Fatima couldn't believe what she had just heard. Her father had killed someone. A boy, a young boy looking for his family. And her father, Hamid Hassan Kheir Alseed and his uncle Abdal Wahab had killed him; pushed him into a room and beaten him to death. Then they had loaded the body onto a donkey cart, covered it with empty sacks and pushed it through the streets in broad daylight all the way down to the river. Fatima was still reeling from Sawsan's death, and the old woman's sudden appearance at Mohamed's funeral. The whole village was in turmoil and rumours were rife. When Mohamed Altahir had called her mother into the deiwan that evening Fatima had thought someone else had died. And it turned out that someone had died, but a long time ago. Thirty-one years ago, to be exact.

Why was her father telling her mother this? And why now?

Mohamed Altahir closed his eyes tightly and rubbed his forehead, opened them again, and took a deep breath.

'It was an accident. We didn't mean for any of it to happen. I didn't mean to ... to hurt anyone.'

'An accident?' Habiba whispered in disbelief.

Her father did not look up.

'But what did you think would happen?! What did you think those criminals would do?'

'I was young, I thought I was doing something important. I was with them at the house when that boy appeared and started making a scene. I thought we were just going to scare him away.'

'By beating him to death and throwing his body in the river?' Habiba threw up her hands. 'How could you ever do such a thing? How could you?'

Mohamed Altahir buried his face in his hands and did not reply. 'He was so tall I did not realise that he was so young.'

Habiba looked up at Mohamed Altahir in despair.

'I suppose I knew. There were whispers,' she said quietly, 'that the Kheir Alseeds had been involved in something, but no one had any proof. I remember as a small girl overhearing my father telling my uncles that a strange boy had come to the village looking for Hassan Kheir Alseed's house. Only a few people saw him that afternoon. It would have been unimportant, except that Hassan had already died then. And the boy looked a bit strange; he looked like the Kheir Alseeds, but also, not like them.'

Fatima's parents looked at each other, as if seeing one another for the first time.

'I heard about the strange woman near the river, too.

But then she too disappeared, and people said she was a witch of some sort. I wasn't sure that you were involved. But of course I knew that you and Hamid Kheir Alseed were once good friends, and then you weren't.'

Mohamed Altahir stood up. 'I don't know why we did it, except that we knew no one would care, because this boy and his mother were not one of us.'

Habiba was still sitting. 'Allah has punished you enough,' she said. 'Only He punished all of us when Khalid died.' There was a long pause.

'It should not have been Khalid at the bottom of the river,' Fatima heard her mother add quietly.

Twenty-One

Every night, Nyamakeem replayed the moment she had given in and told her son who his family was. She kept replaying it and stopping right before that moment. Changing the ending and saying the words: your father's family is far, far away from here. Somewhere we couldn't reach them, and they couldn't reach us. I don't know where they are. And then everything would have been fine.

But she couldn't change the ending, and here she was: childless and alone.

When Nyamakeem looked into Sulafa's anguished face that afternoon, she saw herself. She felt her own heart breaking at the loss of the child, the son of the man who had killed her son. She looked at Sulafa and felt the fire in her heart die.

A life for a life, she told Hajja Allagiya.

Her business with them was done.

❧

Fatima ran through the dark streets, the only thought in her head that of getting as far away from her home as possible. She passed Fathiya bit Zainab's house, the Elhadis', her in laws', stumbled over the rock that Mustafa Hamid used to prop behind the wheels of his donkey cart, got back up and ran past the funeral tent outside Sawsan's house. She turned corners blindly, running away and upward, across the empty plot where the neighbourhood boys played football, behind the small mosque that had been locked for the night after Isha prayers, until she reached the abandoned pigeon house where she stopped and leaned over, breathing heavily, and vomited. Legs shaking, she tried to stand up but couldn't and instead half-crawled around the crumbling building and sunk to the ground behind it. She opened her mouth to breathe in more air, but instead vomited again, this time on her own clothes. She breathed in and out, and gradually her breaths turned into cries. Her mind was churning, full of white noise. She felt like she was falling through the air but stuck in place.

She shut her eyes and buried her face in her arms, rocking back and forth. The sounds around her, which she had heard all her life and knew like her own heartbeat, now sounded foreign to her ears. The sky above had expanded, becoming wider and farther out of reach. She didn't recognise her surroundings anymore. It was as if she had fallen asleep and woken up in a completely different world.

Everything was possible. Even the impossible.

Fatima heard movement behind her and turned around and saw Sadig standing on the road below the pigeon house, frowning up at her in the receding light.

'Why are you running down the street like a boy? And at this time? It's almost dark. And there are scorpions everywhere.'

Fatima could have asked him how he had found her this far from home, but she didn't care. She turned away from him and buried her head in her arms again. She heard Sadig shuffle around, mumbling some vague condolences for Sawsan's passing away. Then his movement came closer and Fatima looked up to see that he had climbed up and sat down a short distance away from her. If she felt terrible, Sadig looked worse; his clothes were dirty and crumpled, his feet black in their muddy sandals, and his head was bare. She looked down at her own vomit-covered dress, vaguely aware of how she smelled and looked. This was probably no way to look in front of a groom.

They sat in silence, staring at the ground between them.

'I came to your house to talk to my uncle and saw you leave,' Sadig said, as if answering her unasked question.

Fatima didn't reply. She wished he would go away.

'Did you have some kind of an argument?'

Fatima rolled her eyes.

'Really, Sadig? I hardly think that's your business.'

Sadig suddenly kicked off his sandal and Fatima gasped, raising her arm to block the blow. Instead, Sadig flung his sandal on the ground, crushing the tiny scorpion that was creeping between the stones towards them with its tail curved over its back. Sadig looked down at Fatima with bemusement.

'Did you think I was going to hit you?'

Fatima lowered her arm with a huff and turned away again. She had come here to be alone and clear her head. She needed to think about what she had just heard, about her life after this unwelcome revelation. She didn't have time for Sadig and his nonsense. She heard him pick his sandal up and sit back down.

'Was it about that woman who appeared at the Kheir Alseed's this afternoon?' Sadig asked quietly.

'You knew about that too?' Fatima exclaimed, looking up. 'How?'

'I didn't know about anything. What was it about her that was so upsetting you ran away from home at this hour?'

It was now so dark that Fatima could only see Sadig's silhouette against the rocky wall behind him. She looked at the hunched shoulders and the bent head as he modestly avoided looking directly at her even in the low light, his serious tone in stark contrast with the smug Sadig who had been showing off his swimming skills the last time they met. What was he really doing here? Why had he followed her? Why did he care what was bothering her so much? Fatima realised that she knew almost nothing about this man, and he was supposed to be her husband before the year was out.

She remembered Sawsan joking about how her fiancé wouldn't be able to find her in a crowd of women, just two days ago. It was a joke but not far from the truth: there was little to no mixing between men and women before marriage. The suitor's mother and sisters were the ones who chose the potential bride and did the inspection: checking the girl's hair, her legs, the way she walked, any scars or disfigurements. But sometimes, as with Fatima and Sadig, there was no need even for that: their fathers being brothers, their marriage had been decided from birth. Fatima was aware that she was envied by many of the village girls for her 'luck', with Sadig's relative wealth from his travels, but she had given little thought to anything positive about their betrothment. But with the storm of events that she was caught up in, she did not find it strange that she suddenly wanted to let Sadig in.

'That woman was married to Hassan Kheir Alseed, the one who had been in the South. They had a son.'

She was struggling to get the words out and to block out what she had heard earlier at the same time.

'They had a son together and the Kheir Alseeds killed him because he wanted to collect his inheritance.'

Suddenly, Fatima felt an intense rage, a fireball of anger in her chest, a fountain of bitter bile pushing up her throat. So much nonsense decreed from generation unto generation of what 'should' be done, what was 'right', how things should be. So much nonsense that determined each person's worth and where they were placed in the hierarchy of life. Who was the highest, who was lower than who, and who was at the very bottom, where their very right to life was dictated by those above them. She thought about how the Kheir Alseeds, while rich and powerful in their village, were unknown and irrelevant beyond their village's borders. Yet their relative superiority gave them the power to wreak havoc on the lives of the two women who had been unlucky enough to cross their paths. The same superiority was tolerated – and indeed, bolstered – by those around them, and by the conditions they had been lucky enough to be born into.

Sadig shifted his weight and re-crossed his ankles. He hadn't said anything while Fatima was talking – or crying – and his face was impassive.

'What is it exactly that you're so upset about?'

Fatima was taken aback.

'What do you mean? How can I not care about someone dying?'

'That's not what I asked. I asked, what are you upset about exactly? Are you upset that someone died? Or why the death happened?'

Fatima stared at Sadig and opened her mouth to scream at him that it was all of those things and more: it was the betrayal, it was the living of a lie, of false modesty and piety, it was the injustice heavily handed down with no right. It was the punishment that had fallen on her brother because of what someone else had done. It was her own loss that was never acknowledged and how the loss of a sibling is never considered equal to the loss of a parent. It was all the questions that had no answers and all the questions that were never asked.

But she said none of those things. Because she could not answer Sadig. What was she upset about? Other than what this discovery meant to her own life?

'It's a terrible thing that someone died,' Sadig said with a sigh. 'But I can't say I'm really surprised. So that woman who came this afternoon is the same one that people have sometimes seen in the village? And she was once married and shunned by the Kheir Alseeds? We both know that there have been stories of villagers having wives from the South and West, Fatima. But how many have you seen here?'

'I know that, but –'

'And if Southerners did live here among us, would us villagers mix with them? Would we accept them as our own? Would the villagers you know have married their sons or daughters? Fatima,' Sadig said, as he turned to face her directly, 'would you marry your children – our children – to one of them?'

Fatima turned her face away from him. Bile pushed at her throat, threatening to come out. Briefly, she wished it would and that she would vomit over Sadig's smug face.

'You know we have no say about who we marry around here.'

'And you know what I mean.'

Fatima closed her eyes. This wasn't what they were supposed to be talking about. This was beyond the point. This wasn't about her or what she would or wouldn't do.

'You wouldn't, and neither would I.'

'I wouldn't because I couldn't, not because I thought we were too good for them,' Fatima slashed out. 'No one would let me. My family would disown me for just thinking about it, because no one would marry *my* children and grandchildren because of who their parent was, and that's not something I could live with. I would think it was ridiculous that the thing standing between me and the man I wanted to marry was his tribe! And I wouldn't kill you!'

'You wouldn't, maybe. Or you wouldn't *now*. But what about later? What about when you're older and your blacks and whites aren't so black and white? What if you felt threatened because something was going to be taken away from you?'

'Ya Sadig, stop talking circles around me. Just say whatever it is you want to say.'

'What I want to say is that I know all this is bad, but it is what it is. Yes, it's wrong, but neither of us can change it. And why get so upset because it doesn't make a difference to you anyway, to be honest. You don't love a man from a different tribe. The wrongs in this didn't make a difference to you until now, anyway.'

'That's not true!'

But wasn't it? Fatima reluctantly allowed Sadig's unwelcome words to settle down in her mind long enough to think about them. It was like being forced to drink something she hated. What he was saying was true, but also not true. How often had she thought about how the deep-seated racism they lived in? She couldn't remember. But it wasn't because it didn't matter, it just never came up. And it never came up because there was never an 'event', or 'something that happened' that stirred a discussion.

She thought of Nasima who passed by their house several times a week. She always found a glass of black tea and a bowl of fava beans waiting for her. Habiba would sit across from her chatting about whatever news there was while she tended to her pots and pans. But Nasima always sat on the small, low roped bed in the tukul or in the alley where they hung the washing. She never sat inside the house or on one of the grand metal beds in the women's yard with their flowered bedsheets and the doilies on the tables. Fatima found it difficult to picture Habiba ordering Nasima to sit outside, or not allowing her to come inside the house. Nasima must be the one who would choose her place of seating, because she knew where she was expected to sit.

And Habiba never invited her in – at least, not to the best of Fatima's knowledge. Nor had Fatima ever found the whole thing strange or unacceptable. She had never invited Nasima in either. Whereas Zamzam, the young widow who was as poor as Nasima if not worse off, always sat inside the kitchen or the shaded verandah when she passed by, and fitted in comfortably with the other women in the yard when visiting in a more official manner.

'But they killed her son.'

'And that was wrong. I'm not defending that, and never will. I don't defend their turning him away and denying him his inheritance either. But I'm not surprised, and I doubt anyone else around here would be. Everyone has their secrets.'

Fatima leaned back against the pigeon house. Sadig was right, she was unable to deny it, and she hated that.

Sadig pushed himself wearily off the ground and slipped his feet into his sandals, dusting the back of his jallabiya.

'It's late, Fatima. Come on, I'll walk you home.'

She stood up slowly. She felt trapped. This new reality was not a place that she knew. It was not a place that she could call home anymore. She turned her back to him and looked down at her hand holding the folded envelope, now crushed and splattered.

That afternoon, she had returned from Mohamed's funeral to find a visitor in the front yard, waiting for her. Sit Asha, the butcher's wife and her schoolteacher was sitting on one of the metal beds, her eyes puffy and her appearance rumpled. Her tob was clean but wrinkled, her face was tired, and her hair – usually shiny and brushed straight – was a mess with bits of leaves and twigs in it. Her face was framed with ash where she had neglected to wash properly. She got up as Fatima pushed the door shut and approached her, and the two embraced and wept. Sit Asha and her husband's families had owned small plots of citrus trees and a modest number of livestock. All had been wiped out. Also, Sawsan had been one of her favourite students.

Fatima let go and bade Sit Asha to sit down so she could get her some water, but Sit Asha wasn't staying.

'I must get back home. I haven't seen my children since yesterday evening and don't even know what they ate, if anything at all. I just passed by to give you this.'

Fatima looked down and her heart skipped a beat as she saw the envelope. She reached out for it and turned it over, running her fingers over the Ministry of Education's stamp on the back.

'I remembered the post would arrive today or tomorrow. I passed by the school earlier and found it there.'

She reached out and held Fatima's face and smoothed her hair.

'I'm sure you'll find good news inside. You really are the cleverest girl in this village. If the University of Khartoum is where you're planning to go, they will be lucky to have you.'

Fatima had shut the door behind Sit Asha and rushed through the house looking for Habiba so that they could open the envelope together. She had heard her parents' voices coming from the deiwan. Now, looking down at the unopened envelope in her hands, Fatima knew that regardless of what she would find in there, her life had already changed.

∞

Sulafa stood in front of the shack in the darkness of the mountains, the wind from the open dunes blowing noisily between the crumbling walls of the ghost houses behind her. Far away, the calls for Isha prayers travelled towards her in waves from the village. She shivered in the light tob she was wearing with the short-sleeved house dress underneath. She still had her plastic slippers on, which were covered in Sara's dried blood. The zinc door creaked open and the old woman slowly stepped out. She didn't seem surprised to see Sulafa standing there, shivering in the dark. Nyamakeem turned around to look at her house. She stood there for a long time, and Sulafa watched her quietly, unsure what to say, unsure what she was even doing there. She had no recollection of making the decision to come.

She watched as the old woman reached inside and pulled the door slowly shut, then turned around to face her. She was holding a small bag in her hand. Sulafa had nothing. The two mothers who were mothers no more looked at each other for a while. Then, Nyamakeem reached into her bag and pulled out a folded cloth. It was a man's white cotton shawl, with two dark blue stripes along the edges. She shook it slowly open and lifted it to her face, smelling it. Then she held it out to Sulafa, who took it and wrapped it around her shoulders.

Nyamakeem did not ask any questions, nor did she appear uncomfortable with the unexpected company. Silently, she turned and leaned her staff on the wall of her house. She shouldered the small bag, made smaller with the removal of the shawl, and walked slowly towards Sulafa. Together, the two women turned and walked into the night.

⌒〜

Dr Mustafa stood blinking in the bright morning sunshine, a heavy briefcase in one hand and an aging box file tucked under his arm.

'You're here for what?' the boy asked him again over his shoulder as he measured out some milk into a pot. His donkey stood motionless beside him under the weight of the large steel pails hanging on both sides.

'To examine the sick animals,' Dr Mustafa said. He tried to talk and hold his breath at the same time; the smell of fresh milk nauseated him.

The boy handed the pot back to the woman waiting behind the house door and turned to face the veterinarian. He looked him up and down, taking in the shiny shoes, the leather belt that tucked his ironed shirt into his ironed trousers. His eyes traced the straight moustache that sat diligently under the vet's nose, not a single hair poking out of place.

'The animals that died you mean? The ones we burnt two days ago?'

Dr Mustafa didn't much care for the boy's sarcastic tone and had no interest in explaining to him how the civil service worked and the procedures that needed to be followed. What difference did two days' wait make? It wasn't as if this village had anything important going on.

'Just point me in the direction of the imam's house,' he said, irritably.

'Hop on, I'll take you there. It's my next stop anyway.'

Dr Mustafa tried to maintain some of his haughtiness as he perched on top of the donkey, his left arm wrapped tightly around the briefcase and box file while the right hand held onto the ropes holding the milk buckets in place. The boy clicked his tongue and walked ahead of him and the donkey trotted obediently behind, the vet rocking side to side and feeling his dignity wilting along with his moustache under the bright, hot sunshine.

ACKNOWLEDGMENTS

A Mouth Full of Salt was born out of a story I was told years ago, about a child who had died while in the care of his grandparents. It started as a short story, then evolved over the years into what it finally became, through the support of many people. Without their contributions it may have never seen the light.

I want to thank my parents for everything, including driving us every Thursday evening to House of Prose to buy books for as long as I can remember, filling in for the absence of a public library and building the literary foundation without which I wouldn't have written a single word. And my sisters and brothers for bearing with me through the ten thousand drafts of this and other pieces of work, providing their honest feedback, assuring me that I'm not that terrible at writing and putting up with me as a sister. Thank you Gafer for lending me the valuable memories of your childhood and opening a window for me into a time and place that would have otherwise not been accessible, and for babysitting. Thank you Ali, Othman and Adnooni for giving my life meaning.

Thank you to all the people who believed in me over the years and directly and indirectly led me to being published: Lamya, Rania Taifour, Marcus, Omnia Shawkat, Rod Usher, Amal Osman, Djamila Hamid; and Ali Ramram, and Ms Leila Aboulela and Nana Ekwa Brew-Hammond for putting up with my endless questions and always offering their endless support. Thank you to my South Sudanese friends who provided valuable feedback, information and friendship: Ruot, Emmanuel, Joshua and Mr. Ramadan Awow, and Deng Aling for pointing out the inconsistencies in the manuscript even though he thought it was a terrible story. Thank you, Elizabeth Briggs at Saqi Books, for believing in *A Mouth Full of Salt* and for pushing me to bring it to its full potential.

And of course, my undying gratitude to Karen Jennings, Robert Peet, Hamza Koudri and Rachel Edwards for believing in *A Mouth Full of Salt* enough to grant it first place in The Island Prize, allowing me to proudly represent Sudan for the first time, and changing my life forever.